THE NEW BIZARRO AUTHOR SERIES

PRESENTS

KITTEN

G. Arthur Brown

Eraserhead Press
Portland, OR

THE NEW BIZARRO AUTHOR SERIES
An imprint of Eraserhead Press

ERASERHEAD PRESS
205 NE BRYANT
PORTLAND, OR 97211

WWW.ERASERHEADPRESS.COM

ISBN: 1-62105-065-3

Copyright © 2012 by G. Arthur Brown

Cover art copyright © 2012 by Nihil & Rat
www.nihil-and-rat.com

All rights reserved. No part of this book may be reproduced or transmitted in any form or by any means, electronic or mechanical, including photocopying, recording, or by any information storage and retrieval system, without the written consent of the publisher, except where permitted by law.

Printed in the USA.

You hold in your hands now a book from the New Bizarro Author Series. Normally, Eraserhead Press publishes twelve books a year. Of those, only one or two are by new writers. The NBAS alters this dynamic, thus giving more authors of weird fiction a chance at publication.

For every book published in this series, the following will be true: This is the author's first published book. We're testing the waters to see if this author can find a readership, and whether or not you see more Eraserhead Press titles from this author is up to you.

The success of this author is in your hands. If enough copies of this book aren't sold within a year, there will be no future books from the author published by Eraserhead Press. So, if you enjoy this author's work and want to see more in print, we encourage you to help him out by writing reviews of his book and telling your friends.

In any event, hope you enjoy KITTEN by G. Arthur Brown. Incidentally, it was the only NBAS book I accepted this year. Kevin Shamel had better luck, as he took the other five.

—Kevin L. Donihe, Editor

This book is dedicated to A. E. Iou, whose story it shall always remain, and to Gail, who had the courage to admit at 72 that she still didn't know what she wanted to be when she grew up.

Additional thanks to Mr. Nihil (www.nihil-and-rat.com—for both his artwork and for some pan-weird story elements), Donny Baumer, Vince Kramer, Ray Fracalossy, Jon Konrath, Matt Hegdahl, Reggie Smalls, Sean Tigert, Richard B. Jr., Emily Simon, Todd Manza, Kim Davis, David A. Hill, Dave Hutchinson, Robert Valding, Mark Leake & Dire Wit Films, Patrick Rose, Tracy Snow, Jeff "JyVy" VanderMeer, Elaine Walker, The Late Peter Cook, and Peter Crates. And of course to Kevin L. Donihe, the hardest working man in Bizarro.

PART ONE:

A TERRIBLE DAY

CHAPTER ONE

Amaand was having one of those dreams that was more like watching a movie. She was a passive observer to the events that transpired, reacting to and judging them, but not able to affect them, even in the unconscious manner of dreams. A representative of the Tax Board sat behind a large, institutional desk in a power suit, sipping her latte. Her visitor was an elderly man with a long gray beard and a yarmulke on a wooly head of hair. Briefly, he described his early days in Israel and his service in Mossad, as well as his expatriation to the United States in the late 70s. He explained that he was back again this year to renegotiate his taxes. "Sir, we don't personally negotiate taxes with private citizens. There is a tax code," said the representative, bored. "Yes, yes!" the man said and began to laugh. "This is what they all say!" He started to pull strange objects from his attaché case—small mannequin heads with what seemed to Amaand to be hairpieces on each side of the head, like bizarre locks for the punk rock Hasid. Perhaps these were his awards for excellent service to the State of Israel. She didn't know much about Jews and had never stopped to consider until this moment what kind of awards they might receive and for what. Each head had a year printed on it: 1978, 1979, 1981, 1984… Four of them were set on the desk before Amaand realized they were not hairpieces for humans, but the ears of lap dogs and bits of adjoining fur. The old man was threatening the tax board. If they did not adjust his tax rate down, their dogs would wind up trophies like all those of defiant bureaucrats in the past. A little boy with an ice cream cone walked up and started petting the ears of a Pomeranian. "Mommy!" said the boy, melting ice cream leaking from his mouth. His voice sounded like that of her son.

"Mommy! There's something wrong with my kitten!" Amaand realized she had dozed off again at the kitchen table, probably just a side effect of her most recent meds. Her son, Trevor, was calling for her. She walked into the dimly lit, overly yellow family room at a casual pace because she knew that whatever he was complaining about had been blown out of proportion. She placed her hands on her hips, atop her stiff floral apron, and gave a cursory look at Trevor in his Pirate Piet t-shirt and then at his pitiable pet. She saw three things wrong with the kitten, two of which she had noticed before. First of all, Trevor's kitten was not a kitten but actually some kind of squirrel. The silly boy loved the thing so much that she had never had the heart to tell him the truth. Second, the squirrel was deformed and probably also retarded. It had very sharp claws, which may have been why Trevor still believed it to be a kitten, and it usually did nothing but walk in circles all day. It also had no fear of man and was unable to climb trees. Not a prime example of squirrelhood (and certainly not any sort of example of kittenhood). Third, and this was the only news to Amaand, it was vomiting up stamps from all over the world, quite a nice collection of them at that. Sadly, she saw immediately they had all been postmarked so she couldn't even use the American ones to mail anything.

Of all the things this kitten could be vomiting into existence, she found stamps to be particularly annoying and un-useful. She had given the kitten to Trevor only to irritate Ted, her husband. The pathetic animal now simply reminded her of a failed marriage and was a constant nuisance. "If your kitten doesn't start earning his keep pretty soon, I'll need to start charging you for his food," she told Trevor.

"He can't help it, Mommy. He wants to throw up something useful. I know it!"

"And how do you know that, Trevor? You are six and only in your second year of veterinary school. When you've got a piece of paper that says Kitten Psychologist on it, then we can talk."

He grimaced, dug his hand into his pocket and pulled out a folded note. She snatched it from his hand, unfolding it with caution so as not to damage the yellowed, brittle paper. In calligraphy, it read: Kitten Psychologist. "Where did this come from?" She asked him angrily. She already knew the answer.

"From Grandfather's trunk."

"And who goes into Grandfather's trunk?" she asked him.

He knew what to say. "Only dead boys and girls, Mommy. Only dead boys and girls go in Grandfather's trunk, because it isn't safe in there for live little children."

"Then how did you get this paper?"

"A dead girl came out last night to pet my kitten. Her eyes were black and her hair was black. I told her that she had no right to touch my pet, but she said that she was trained to take care of animals, and she gave me this piece of paper to prove it. So then I let her touch my kitten and *this* happened!" He pointed at a pile of at least three dozen stamps, now representing nations from every inhabited continent.

"I'll have to have a chat with the old bastard and set this all straight." She hated talking to her father-in-law, especially now that he was dead. But Trevor was too upset and stupid to sort things out for himself. A mother's work required sacrifices from time to time. She popped a small yellow pill and was off.

CHAPTER TWO

Her father-in-law was pissed, of course, when Amaand disturbed him. He called his place The Crypt, but it was actually a condo on the East Side. "Hello, Marvin. How is death treating you?" The question was a mistake.

"Death… death. Well, Amaand, let me tell you a little something about death." He looked good, considering his state. She thought he almost appeared better than in life. Vaguely handsome for a dead man, he sat wearing his glasses and smoking a pipe, on a small settee with ivory inlay. "Death is not something I knew of as a child. I kicked my ball and played with dogs all day long. It wasn't until I saw my hound, Helios, die—hit by a car—that I came to the realization that death was a force to be reckoned with. My father's money kept most tribulations at bay, which is why I could afford to kick my ball and play with dogs all day long. Work was unknown to me." He stood up and walked over to a picture window that had once overlooked a beautiful wooded park, but which now overlooked a small industrial complex that manufactured Plexiglas fixtures for a major retail chain. "In my teens, I thought I could defeat death—beat him at his own game. I drove fast, drank like an Arctic drinking fish, jumped from second story balconies to escape overprotective older brothers, outran or outwitted guard dogs. All that time, I never considered that I would perish. It wasn't until my late thirties that I began to realize that, like my beloved Helios, I too would die. I would turn into corruption. I would become like unto earth. Filthy." He pursed his

KITTEN

lips, took the pipe from them and stared at his feet. "In my 60s, that's when I began to lose the fear. I stopped watching what I ate, stopped exercising. I bought another fast car that I drove at top speed. I knew that my body was decaying out from under me. And I began to think of death as a friend, you know? An end to my suffering."

He must have heard Amaand snort sardonically, though she tried to conceal it as best she could below the sound of fiddling in her purse to find pills. He looked at her, eyes dead but face very much alive: "When I first found myself dead I imagined that it was all over, my work done. But when I thought about my family, I didn't want to let go. So I walked the streets and, right away, the people there shunned me. They knew I was no longer one of them. And I feared the grave... oh, how I feared it. I drank and took pills—a few of the doctors would still see me. Eventually, however, I realized there was no use in fighting it. I was only protracting a horrible experience for my loved ones. Then, and only then, did I let them bury me." He sat down again, sighed. "You can't imagine how horrible that is, really, Amaand. The claustrophobia, the dark, the stifling lack of air. Waiting for the wood of the casket to decay to the point where the worms can find your flesh, their food, which you have been depriving them of for far too long. *I had deprived them of...* not you, Amaand. I don't mean to sound like I'm talking about you. But you'll find your own method to sort yourself out."

She looked at him with puzzlement.

"I'm just talking," he continued. "But after the first year in the grave, I decided to buy this condo. I know I could have left that money to Ted and you to take care of little Trevor, but I'm nearly in my prime. Now, I see that death is not a release. It's a contract. A contract with oneself, to finally go and do the things you'd put off in life." He regarded her sternly with a quick turn of his head. "I know what you are thinking. 'Marvin, you had a condo before you died.' And yes, Amaand, you are right. But I didn't have *this* condo."

Her ears pricked up. "This condo? What do you mean?"

"This condo offers me things that no other condo could." He looked at her, knowingly. She looked back, unknowingly.

"Could you please elaborate?"

He raised his arm slowly, as if the motion pained him. Then he quickly snapped his fingers and pointed out the window to the pool below. "The only pool in the area that the dead are allowed to swim in. It has special chemicals added to aid in… preservation."

Amaand furrowed her brow. "Let me get down to brass tacks, Marvin. The boy has been into your trunk and he came out with this." She produced the folded note from a white handbag. Marvin took the note, which he studied deliberately and cautiously, taking far longer than it could possibly take to read two words.

"Are you sure he went into the trunk?" he said, finally.

"He told me one of your victims brought it to him as collateral or something so she could pet his kitten."

Yawning, Marvin scratched his chin absently. "I don't see any reason to doubt him."

"But we put a spectral gate on there—"

He scoffed. "Those things are about as effective as the gizmos you plug into wall outlets to keep bugs away. Believe me; since I've been dead I have had to deal with a few of those gates. They're annoying, but they'll hardly stop a determined revenant from going about his or her business. And the dead have far more business than you'd believe."

KITTEN

"Why do you think she'd want to pet his kitten? And it isn't a kitten, by the way."

He marched over to his bar and tugged the stopper from a tall, green bottle. "The dead love a good contradiction. Plus, there's a real shortage of cuddly things beyond the grave. I've seen dead men with night crawlers for pets, that's how desperate they get for affection." He took a long pull of whatever foul concoction occupied the strange vessel, something only the dead drink. "And I suppose the vomiting has already ensued."

"You bet it has. *Stamps of the world*. No luck comes my way."

Marvin adjusted his glasses, seeming as if he were again pursuing a scientific inquiry. He had always been one of those quasi-hunky scientists that one only sees in old science fiction films. "Are you really put off by the... disgorgements?"

"I am put off by this, this, this *kitten* that no longer serves any purpose."

"Doesn't the boy enjoy having the kitten?"

"Well, sure. But you wouldn't believe how much food this little bugger can put away. I mean, it puts Ted to shame, and you've seen him wolf down a rack of ribs after he's worked up an appetite in the moon bounce. And now, what, with all the vomiting..."

"Patience, Amaand. Eventually it has to cough up a rare and valuable stamp. Law of averages."

"I need a quicker solution."

"You really want to get rid of this thing?"

She nodded slowly, seriously.

Marvin tapped his fingers on the oak bar-top—each in sequence, starting with the pinky and ending with the index. He did this once, twice, ten times. Then spoke: "I know a guy. A collector." He shuffled over to his desk, hunched over and spent a while rooting through a Rolodex that he must have had since the early 80s. He finally pulled out a business card, which he tossed Frisbee-style at Amaand, a woman not known for her cat-like reflexes. It hit her in the forehead and fell into her lap. He regarded her with a smirk. "Now fuck off and let me enjoy my dead years."

CHAPTER THREE

"Hello?" said a voice as dry as death.

"Hello, this is Amaand Graynes." She had phoned him on her cell as she drove back home. "Dr. Graynes, my father-in-law, gave me this number. He said you were a collector."

"Well." He coughed directly into the receiver before proceeding: "What do you have for me?"

"A kitten that's not a kitten. Coughing up stamps. Pretty nice ones."

"How did your *kitten* come to be coughing up stamps? That's pretty rare, I must admit." He now sounded interested.

"Well, one of the dead girls came out of Marvin's trunk and petted the thing."

He breathed heavily, almost obscenely. "And you witnessed this yourself?"

"No, my son Trevor did."

"How old is the boy?"

"Six. Listen, what's that got to do with—"

"I'm the Collector. Just leave the questions to me. If you don't mind, I've got a few more." A sound, something like the sucking of a lozenge, filled the next few seconds. Then: "This girl from the trunk, did your boy describe her at all?"

"Not really. Not very well. Black hair, I seem to recall."

"Is she in good condition?"

"Probably. If you know my father-in-law, you should know he spent a lot of time preserving those kids. But Trevor didn't say anything about her *state*."

"She's got the touch, though. That's interesting, wouldn't you say?"

Amaand didn't know what to say, so she just cleared her throat.

"Did he say she was pretty? Some of these dead kids are hideous. It's only every once in the bluest of moons that you run across a keeper. A zombie-doll, as my colleagues have started calling them."

Amaand said very loudly, "She's not the problem."

"I collect many things, lady." There was an uncomfortable pause. "I've just got a few more questions. Your boy… what does he look like?"

Amaand froze for a moment, tried to focus on the task of driving. "Well… how about I call you back once I get more details from Trevor?"

He laughed, but she could tell he was holding his phone away from his face to make it less obvious. "I'll be waiting. I'm really looking forward to meeting your menagerie. Ta-ta."

CHAPTER FOUR

She returned to her small but comfortable suburban home in a bad mood but with hopes high. Then Trevor had to ruin everything: "Daddy's on TV again, Mommy."

She looked at their widescreen, at the flickering image of her estranged husband as he sweated and tried to convince viewers that he was in the right, she in the wrong. On a whiteboard he had even drawn a Venn diagram, the intersection labeled "Things we both did wrong." Her circle was so full of writing that he'd actually written other things outside it and drawn little arrows indicating they really should be inside her half of the diagram. The reason that was written the largest was this: "She got my son a kitten." Slightly smaller print underneath it read: "The kitten she got was not a kitten."

"I am allergic. There is nothing I can do," her husband said from the television screen. "If she could only understand the science behind it, maybe she would get rid of the kitten and take me back. I cannot live in a house with that kitten. She is completely in the wrong. I urge everyone to write her letters. I urge any scientists watching to explain the science to her on the back of a postcard." He held up a picture of Trevor when he was just three years old and wearing a sailor suit. "I love my son. I have this picture of him. Does anyone doubt that I love him?" He looked intensely at the camera and waited. Amaand wondered if he actually expected a response.

"Daddy loves me!" yelled Trevor. He lay down on his belly and propped his head up with his arms to watch the rest of the paid infomercial his father was wasting so much money making.

"Yes of course, dear. But I don't love Daddy. He loves you, but he's also insane right now. Something to do with the alignment of the planets."

Trevor kicked his feet. "He says it's the kitten."

Amaand stared as hard as she could at the kitten that was not a kitten. It did not explode, no matter how many times she silently repeated "explode, damn you" in her head. It curled up next to Trevor and vomited more stamps onto the family room carpet. Amaand took another pill out of her purse and swallowed it without anything to wash it down.

"Let me tell you all something," said the weary Ted from the television. "My wife Amaand once hid under her father's bed for two hours to see him naked after he got out of the shower."

Amaand threw her purse at the screen. "That's not true and you know it, Ted! We read that in a book of people's confessions revealed by a disgruntled priest!" She forced herself to calm down. She wouldn't let him drive her crazy; that had to be what he was trying to do. His paid advertisements for his blamelessness could be seen several times a day and on all the major stations. *Hot Teen Drama* had even been preempted earlier in the week to make way for Ted's rifling through old photo albums and explaining how Amaand had managed to ruin each and ever memory frozen therein. She wanted to take the pathetic man-boy as he slept and smother him until all his impotent rage was as muted as the color of the outdated suit he wore on the broadcast.

"Mommy, Daddy can't hear you. He's inside TV."

"He's not inside the TV, Trevor. He's *on* the TV."

Trevor stood up and looked at the top of the set. He saw only a DVD player, and on top of that, a small plastic figurine made to look like a family-friendly gangster that he had gotten from a vending machine. He leaned very close to the little man in the red bandana and whispered, "Daddy, is that you?"

The figurine laughed silently to itself.

"Trevor," said Amaand, "don't make me smack sense into you."

On the screen, a well-known television personality appeared from off-camera. He looked and sounded a lot like Dick Cavett, but that was a coincidence. "Ted, you are doing a great job, but I wonder if we might go to my studio next door so I can do a fun interview with you. I bet the audience would love that."

Ted looked confused, but somewhat relieved. "Yes, okay. Change of format. Great."

The Dick Cavett-looking celebrity looked straight into Camera A (but Camera B was the one in use) and said, "We'll be right back after this short commercial." And it was a very short commercial. It's the one where the boy, approximately two years of age, is hanging from a second story gutter, moaning, "Mom. Help, Mom," very quietly. You have to get really close to the speaker or turn your set's volume all the way up in order to hear him clearly. It's only 15 seconds long, but that time seems to stretch on, because it looks as if he is about to fall at any second (giving him 15 opportunities to do so). Then, you can see something start to approach the window right above him. His mother? Someone to the rescue? No, it's a large logo for Baby-Falls brand butt-bumpers. They are pads that worrisome parents can affix to their children's diapers to lessen the impact of tottering accidents, and also, presumably, to minutely raise the chances their children will survive a 20-foot drop. The commercial ends with the boy still hanging. Was he rescued in time? Maybe they actually let the child actor fall just to test the product.

It always made Amaand nervous to see this commercial because the boy looked almost exactly like Trevor, and she remembered that Trevor had been two years old at one point.

Trevor, however, would have liked them to turn the commercial into a series. He could imagine about a million variations on the story, most of which involved aliens or kittens or pretty ladies with guns. All of which involved the boy falling to the ground, dying, then getting up and flying into space.

"Ah, we're back," the celebrity said. "I'm here with Ted." He took a sip from a mug of what one could only suppose was coffee, then eyed an index card in his left hand that was probably blank. The whole production looked like a 70s talk show. The seat that Ted sat in was upholstered in gold lame. A zookeeper and his macaw were both asleep in the adjacent chair. They appeared quite comfortable, far more so than Ted who fidgeted and glanced around with a puzzled squint.

The host smiled and said, "Tell me, Ted, what have you been up to recently?"

"Well, just moments ago I was making another infomercial about how my wife is being unreasonable and trying to destroy our family."

"Fantastic. Was that a part that you'd always wanted to play?"

Ted wiped his glistening brow. "Um…"

"I mean, did you have to audition?"

"Um…"

"We call that a joke, Ted. Isn't Ted great, everybody?" A sign lit up and a loud round of applause rang out in the studio and at home, but it was quite obvious there was no one there to watch the impromptu question-answer session. Amaand considered that it could have been demons clapping to torment her, but then settled on the far more likely possibility that this show had been previously taped in Hell for just such an occasion.

A vicious cackle could be heard above the sound of diabolic palms slapping one another.

"So," the celebrity continued once the clapping had faded away, "I think everyone watching is really curious about someone else in your life, someone other than your wicked, evil wife. I'm speaking, of course, of Dr. Marvin Graynes, your father."

"I don't have a lot to say about him."

"I'm sure there's some insight you can offer us on his work. Something that hasn't yet become public knowledge."

Ted took a deep breath and exhaled slowly. "He wasn't the best father."

Ethereal laughter filled the studio. "Oh, Ted, I'm sure we all could guess that much already."

"But, now that he's dead, perhaps he's trying to make up for it, but little things just seem to keep getting worse. For instance, all those children he tried to save from old age won't stay in the trunk anymore, so my wife and I have spent the last few years standing guard at night and sending them back in when they manage to get out. Otherwise, they might disturb our Trevor, who really needs his sleep. He's... a growing boy, and I hate the idea of him being sleepy at school because of my dad. We considered dumping the trunk somewhere in the countryside, but we can't seem to move it out of the corner of the basement without being attacked by spiders."

"Spiders?"

"Yeah, it was some cockamamie idea my dad had that conventional alarms were not nearly as a good a deterrent to burglars as spider attacks. He was—is, as you can probably guess, phobic of spiders. Especially their attacks."

"Are the children he experimented on at all grateful to your father for his work?"

Ted shook his head, furrowed his brow. Uncrossed his legs, then crossed them again. "I don't think so. They are all dead now, and though he gave them vocations—spiritual councilor, alchemical engineer, cat psychologist—they died far too young to make use of their skill-sets. He only used orphans, you know. He also tried to cure them of being orphans, and that's part of what started this whole mess. They might have just all been plain old dead if he hadn't worked so hard. Now they're... unrested. I guess that's what you'd call it. They don't decay, but they don't grow up, either." He added very gravely, "They can't wait to start their professional careers."

"Motivational," the host said, though Ted couldn't tell if he was serious or not. Neither could Amaand. The host himself was only half-sure what he meant, but nobody could see his uncertainty because of his perfectly practiced TV-face.

"This show is boring!" Trevor interjected. "I want the one where Daddy says he loves me to be on. Make it be on!"

"Trevor," Amaand said, "I can't control what insanity your father is choosing to subject the world to at this moment. Right now, he's doing a really boring interview about your grandfather."

"Can the girl come up and watch?"

"The dead girl?"

"Please, Mommy?"

"Oh, alright. I don't see what harm that could do."

The dead girl sat on the couch, while Amaand stood next to her armchair. She glanced occasionally at the chair as if she were about to sit, yet continued to stand and watch the rest of the interview. She didn't want to get too comfortable, considering what was going on with her husband.

On the screen, Ted was being forced to hold the macaw, now awake, while recounting a list of his father's favorite pastimes. "He brunched quite a bit with golfers. You know, old school guys like Palmer and Nicklaus. He built those weird little ships inside bottles. Never understood that one." The macaw tugged at his lapel, and the imaginary audience squealed in delight. "Uh… and he invented some sort of preservative for the recently deceased who won't stay confined to their graves. I think that was his favorite accomplishment, really. He'd spend hours toiling away in the lab, anyway."

The macaw crawled onto the host's desk and started drinking coffee from his mug. "Ted, did he invent the preservative before or after the children died?"

"Well, that's the strange part. He actually discovered the formula because of the children. They were naturally resistant to decay. He only meant for them to not age, to stay at the top of their professions for hundreds of years for, you know, the good of society. But he ended up with dead kids who would stay uncorrupted for hundreds of years. That's why I completely stopped talking to the guy." He winced before adding, "Sure, we still took Trevor to see him on holidays."

"He said my name!" Trevor shouted.

"Shhhh!" the dead girl scolded and gave a disapproving leer.

The host squinted and wrinkled his brow. "Could the dead kids sue your father? If he stole their essence to perfect his formula, they could claim he owes them part of his fortune." The dead girl began writing notes on a cocktail napkin that she'd had balled up in her pocket since the time of her death.

"Don't ask me. I'm not a lawyer," Ted said. That was a flat out lie. He was even wearing his National Lawyer's League tie clip. "Figure of speech," he added as if it meant something.

"That's it; that's all I can take!" Amaand steamed. She looked at the dead girl. "Watch him for a minute for me, okay?" The dead girl nodded. She seemed very easy-going.

CHAPTER FIVE

Amaand stormed outside and over to the next door neighbor's house, a little red-brick rancher with a front yard full of miniature windmills, pinwheels and other wind-activated ornaments. The old woman who lived there had over fifty cats, all imaginary but each with a name and personality that she could describe in detail. "Chester just *loves* to eat bergamot. Nipsy can't stand any citrus, though. But she can sing most standards of the 40s and 50s. Not the words, mind you. But the melody." And so on.

Amaand knocked on the door. Instead of a regular knocking sound, the door produced a squeak like a toy for a dog. "I would have thought it would make a cat toy noise," said Amaand absently to herself as she waited. She tapped her foot and swayed from side to side in the manner of a nervous boxer getting ready to dance with a rich spinster. The door crept open, and the old woman slowly emerged carrying what looked to be a real cat, or what had been in the recent past. "Oh, hello, Amaand. I wasn't expecting company. Don't mind the cats. The males can likely smell your menses." This was news to Amaand, but the thing in the woman's arms remained perfectly still and Amaand didn't care if imaginary cats sniffed all about her person.

"Old woman, my husband is driving me up the wall. I really, really, really need to use your medicine cabinet." The old woman had been prescribed nearly everything over the years, if not for her own ailments, then for those of her cats.

"Go right ahead, dear, but ain't nothing in there except expired meds and Charmkins Band-Aids. I moved all my goodies to the lock-box. And I can't open that but once a day, as the cock crows."

Amaand entered the house, immediately noticing the piercingly sour stench of cat piss. The entire front room, which she couldn't really call a living room because it contained only cat boxes, reeked. She inspected the room quickly and found no sign of any actual cats aside from their waste. How long had the old woman had these filthy litter boxes? Can imaginary cats urinate into the real world? There was no time for these questions, so Amaand made her way down a short hallway, stuccoed inelegantly and hung with ugly portraits of very ugly people, to the bathroom. She quietly muttered, "I've got to find my own method. I hope there's something here that will do the trick."

When she saw the mirror, she froze for a moment in order to make sure she was still real. She raised her hand and gently pawed at her face. "Still there," she reminded herself, and then swung the cabinet open. After a quick scan of the contents, she grabbed at a green bottle labeled Matroheripam, expiration date May 2000. "I just hope this is enough." And she downed the entire bottle.

"Oh, dear. I don't know if you are supposed to take that much," said the old woman, watching from the bathroom doorway.

"Don't worry. Date on it was May 2000. Everything should be fine in a moment." She sat on the toilet. Her head bobbed up and down for a minute or two. Then she slumped over and passed out against the floral patterned wallpaper, which clashed with the pattern on her apron.

CHAPTER SIX

Amaand opened her eyes. She was alone in the old woman's bathroom. She could not be sure what year it was, so she went ahead and snuck out the window just to be safe. The sun made her want a hat. She felt like she was being impelled forward by some unseen force for a purpose not entirely understood. But she needed to be sure *when* she was. She ran up to the mailbox to confirm the date by postmark. May of 2000.

For a minute, she allowed herself to be very proud. Then the reality of the task at hand crept back in. She went home. She worried that she would meet herself. Not because she had the silly notion that the universe would implode if her future and past selves met. If anything, it should be easier for two identical people to exist in very close proximity than simultaneously in distant locales like both London and Albuquerque. That would be asking far too much of the leptons and quarks that comprised her person(s). Rather, she didn't want to run into herself because she would demand an explanation from herself. She just wanted to slip in, talk to her husband and slip back out.

"Hi, Mommy!" said Trevor. He'd spotted her right away. "What were you doing outside?"

"Just checking the mail, honey."

"Did my birthday card come, today, Mommy? I'm minus two!"

She didn't have time for this. "Shush. No one celebrates any birthdays around here until they are at least one year old. You don't even exist yet."

"Maybe not. But I want a card and I want cake, Mommy!"

"You can't want anything, Trevor. You can't even be here yet. Shoo! Skedaddle."

"Aw, you're no fun!" And Trevor sort of faded out of pre-existence. Or so it seemed to Amaand, who was now seeking out her husband, to speak with him before he went insane.

In the kitchen, she saw a familiar face—alive, but not that of her husband. "Why, hello there, Amaand. Such a surprise to see you," her father-in-law said. He sipped at a snifter of brandy, wore sunglasses indoors, exposed quite a bit of chest hair. Next to him stood the dead girl, who was already dead, but only just. The dead girl smiled politely. Her teeth were perfect.

"Marvin, I haven't seen you alive in quite some time."

He laughed. "Looks like you did it."

"Did what?"

"Found your own method. I know you can't be the *you* from now. You must be the *you* from then."

She bugged her eyes out. "Okay, I just travelled several years into the past, so that didn't make a lot of sense to me. Can I have a snort of your brandy?"

"Sure. And have some of what she's having." He pointed to the dead girl, who was eating crackers shaped like kittens that are not kittens.

Amaand took a snort of the brandy and then tried a cracker. "They're delicious. But I really don't have time to chat with you two. I need to find Ted. Do you know where he is?"

"Take a wild guess."

"In the moon bounce?" There was an up inflection at the end, but there really wasn't any question there. She knew damned well he was in the moon bounce.

The dead girl pulled off a ceramic owl's head and presented a cookie to Amaand.

Marvin laughed again. "See. She's getting funnier everyday." He mussed the girl's hair. A large clump came out of her scalp, and he carefully hid it in the ceramic owl cookie jar where no one would think to look for it.

Outside, the moon bounce looked so much newer than she ever remembered it looking. The orange was tomato orange; the blue, insane baby-eye blue. Her husband frolicked gleefully as he was wont to do in those days. She swore she heard him say "Weeeeeeeee!" as she approached.

"Ted," she called to him. He stopped jumping for a moment and looked at her.

"Amaand, is that you? You look different. Older." And then he bit his tongue, because he regretted suggesting she didn't look young anymore and because he hadn't come to a complete state of rest yet, much to the dismay of his jaw.

"Ted, I need to tell you something serious. Please listen to me. And please remember what I tell you."

He raised an eyebrow. "Okay…"

"If in the future we have serious marital problems and you ever have the urge to go on television to rant about it, just remember that there is no chance I will ever love you again after you do it. It will piss me off greatly. Understand?"

He scratched the back of his neck. "Not really. I mean, I understand the words you're using. But I don't know what you mean."

She wobbled a bit. "Just remember what I've told you just now. Promise me."

"I promise," he promised.

Her knee gave way, almost causing her to pitch forward. "I'm feeling a little woozy and I need to lie down now." She fainted, face hitting the grass.

CHAPTER SEVEN

Amaand opened her eyes. She was in an armchair at home but back in the present. She could tell because all Ted's sports memorabilia had been removed from the walls. The television was on and Trevor was watching cartoons. She wanted to thank God it was all over. But as she sat there, she realized it wasn't over at all. She was still experiencing it, and she didn't know why. The kitten was still vomiting up stamps. Trevor was still stupid. Her husband was still somewhere out there, lurking, waiting.

The phone on the table beside her rang. She answered it: "Hello?"

"Hi, Ams. It's me." It was Ted.

"Yeah, I know," she said quietly.

"I just want to say that I understand some things now that maybe I didn't before. When you went back in time, you really showed me what an asshole I can be."

"Did I?"

He breathed heavily. "I know now that the kitten isn't really a kitten. My allergy is an excuse. It represents something else, though."

"To you or to me?"

"It represents what it represents to everyone. It's a concrete symbol."

"Oh really?" she challenged. "If that's so, what does the kitten represent?"

He paused. Cleared his throat. "The kitten represents drugs and desperation. The kitten is the symbol for what you have allowed to come between us and what I cannot stand to face. And even if I did face it, it is that which I cannot repair. There's nothing I can do about the kitten."

"I'm not so sure about that symbol. But don't worry. Everything's going to be okay. You don't need to do anything about the kitten. Your father suggested a collector. That should take care of everything. I don't need the kitten anymore. Anyway, I think that's all really moot now. Trevor and I can… are happy here without you," she hoped.

He sighed. "That breaks my heart to hear. But listen, Amaand, is there anything I can do for you? To make it up to you, even a little?"

She thought for a moment, even though it wasn't necessary. "I'm tired of what you are putting me through. Stop writing this story."

After a long pause, he muttered something distant, as if he had placed his hand over the receiver to speak to someone there with him. Or maybe he was just talking to himself. Amaand could not be sure. Then: "There are too many loose ends. I think it's time for you to meet the Collector."

As if hit in the head with a leather-bound book, she was at a loss for thought, let alone action. "Does he have to…? Are you sure that's a good idea?"

"No, I'm not sure it's a good idea at all. People rarely are sure about that sort of thing. But something needs to happen; it might as well be this." And he hung up.

Something was wrong. She scanned the room, which had taken on a sick, institutional green quality. She blamed the fluorescent bulbs that the government made her buy. Then she realized Trevor was no longer there watching television. "Trevor… baby?" No reply, but a creaking hinge sent a shudder through her body. "Hello?" She stood up, but nearly blacked out as the blood rushed away from her brain. It evidently wished to remain seated, like a wise movie-goer who warns the protagonist not to go in the spooky attic.

The faint spell subsided. It took her eyes a second to adjust. A large blob of color rippled in front of her and gradually formed itself into a man. There was a skeletal gauntness to his face. Hollow eyes stared out of Coke-bottle glasses. A white Panama hat rested atop the thinly haired head, and a great, heaving belly contradicted the lankness of his limbs. In his right arm, he cradled the kitten. With his left hand, he held Trevor fast by the wrist. "Hello, madam," he wheezed. "I'm interested in both of these items and a third—the dead girl you spoke of earlier on the phone. That is, assuming she's not a horrid little troll of a thing. No money in that *at all*!" He laughed a wintry, brittle laugh that sounded about to break off at any moment and fall a hundred feet, smashing the rear window of a sporty little coupe.

Still dazed, Amaand said, "Her teeth are really great."

"Ah," and there was a wicked satisfaction in his voice that made Amaand want to wash out her ears, her eyes, her nose and her mouth.

"Mommy, who is this smelly old guy?" Trevor said. He tried to turn to eye the Collector up, but the man simply squeezed his wrist harder, causing the boy to unleash a quiet "youch."

"He's a stranger, honey. Just be a good boy for a minute and Mommy will handle this."

Upon hearing the word "stranger," Trevor went into a bizarre reverie. His favorite television program, apart from the ones in which his dad talked about him, was *The Oversea Voyages of Pirate Piet*, the ongoing saga of a black pirate captain in a white pirate captain's world. When the title character wasn't busy with pirate things,

KITTEN

he often taught lessons to his young viewers, like special defenses to employ when one should find oneself accosted by a stranger. Having a good memory and little fear, Trevor decided to try Evasive Maneuver No. 3. I cannot commit the exact motions of EM 3 into print for fear that a stranger or two may at some point read this story, and I do not wish to be responsible for putting young children at peril. Suffice it to say that, in a flash, the Collector relinquished his hold on Trevor's wrist to grip his own groin.

Trevor, nimble lad he proved himself to be, sprinted over to and hid behind Amaand's skirt.

Amaand, surprised to hear herself admitting it, said, "Good job, baby! Now, stay there and don't let the man get you again."

The Collector hissed in rage and pain. The kitten, which was not actually a kitten at all, let out a twisted, mewling call. "Before *you* give me any trouble...," the Collector said, fixing his eyes on the kitten. There was a gross click, and his jaw detached as if he were a reptile. Raising his hand to his face, he thrust the kitten into his mouth and swallowed it whole, followed by a cough and a pop as his jaw relocated itself.

"No!" Trevor cried.

"I... I... I...," said Amaand, then she turned to the lamp next to her and grabbed it. "I'm going to throw this lamp at you if you don't leave." She didn't actually give him any time to consider her ultimatum; the lamp was in flight by the time she said "leave."

It sailed through the air toward the man's face and, calmly, he reached out and caught it. He looked it over, turned it upside down and considered the maker's mark. "I've already got one just like it." He let go and sent it crashing to the floor. Little yellow shards of cheap ceramic speckled the goldenrod shag carpeting, creating a pattern that looked rather unlike a kitten, in much the same way the kitten had done.

Amaand was about to make a very desperate move—to run with full force at the Collector—when she saw dark hair and pale skin from the corner of her eye. The dead girl had returned, stalking boldly toward the Collector. She tramped right up to him and stuck out her lily-white hand, palm up, as if waiting to be presented a nickel for a picture show.

"My, my!" the Collector said. "You are a little beaut', aren't you? Look how luminous your skin is, like a glow-in-the-dark toy, like one of those worms I devoured all those years ago."

She implored him with her eyes. He reached out and bent down as if he would start with a kiss on the hand before proceeding to eat the rest of her. But his chance was cut short when she launched her palm toward his face, not to smack him, but to gently caress his cheek.

He flinched, clearly not expecting such affection from the dead girl, who now grinned at him broadly while taking a couple steps backward. He was dumbstruck for a moment as he became nauseated. Then it was clear to him.

Amaand and Trevor were spellbound by the display. It was as if the man were having a seizure, accompanied by nasty croaking sounds. And then his jaws parted again, and something shiny and metal poked free, each jerk bringing a bit more of it into view. His face bent in anguish, not just from the physical discomfort, but also because of the ensuing loss. He spat the object, along with just enough phlegm to insufficiently lubricate its emergence, onto the carpet amidst the shattered lamp. The thing looked suspiciously like a diagram that Amaand had once seen of a device used by 19th Century physicians to measure the

KITTEN

circumference of eyeballs, and was undoubtedly rare and collectable.

"Arrrrgh!" the Collector gasped. Then, pulling himself together momentarily, he shot a hateful look at the dead girl. "I've been a f—" he began, but never got a chance to finish as some other collectible began its short but severe journey up the man's gullet. The Collector was unable to bear it, and doubled over, to rest on his hands and his knees as he produced from his gorge an obsolete prototype for a radio, followed by a jade figurine, followed by one of those strange metal circles doctors used to wear on their heads. The Collector appeared sicker and gaunter after each new item emerged.

"And you see...," said a masculine, worldly voice from the foyer. Amaand searched for the source, but could only make out a vague outline of man standing there in a leisure suit. "...I found my method, as well."

"Grandpa!" shouted Trevor, who began to hop up and down in anticipation of hugs and presents and trips on ocean-going vessels that may or may not have at one time been captained by a certain educational pirate of African blood. For what else are grandfathers useful when you are six?

After a brief survey of the puke-encrusted myriad of curios, Marvin strode to the Collector, who still huddled on the floor on all fours like a sick animal waiting for death, and said plainly, "It looks like all my things are here." Then he kicked him solidly in the face and sent him sprawling into sweet but vomitous oblivion. Marvin wiped off his loafer and turned to Amaand. "Got here just in time, looks like. Any more sickness and you might never have had room for all the—uh—goodies." Trevor squealed and ran to embrace his tall grandfather's kneecaps. With a brief tousling of the hair, Marvin returned the affection.

Then he pointed at the dead girl and said to Amaand, "Ain't she somethin'? And to think my formula was responsible for all this."

Confused and angry, Amaand slapped Marvin in the face. "What the hell was all this about, anyway?"

"You see, Amaand," and Marvin took on a theatrical, authoritative air that made her recall Shakespearean dinner theater, "the man here, lying strewn before us like so much uncased sausage, has taken from me, bit by bit, my valued collectibles, including but not limited to my rare 19th Century medical apparati. The *Collector*, he had called himself, though never again shall he speak his own epithet."

Trevor, having picked up the eyeball-measuring device put it to use and cried out, "It really works, Mommy! I'm size 3.5!"

Marvin continued, "I treasured my belongings, oh how I treasured them! This is one of the reasons I would not accept my death, do you see? So I called in my dim-witted son as a conspirator and we set about the task of undoing this wicked man and regaining my rightful property. Sadly, the best plan we could concoct put you and Trevor in jeopardy. But no harm, no foul." He laughed a little. "You are better off for the effort, I'd say."

"How do you figure?" she demanded.

"Look around you. Do you see that infernal kitten? Or haven't I delivered you from its oppressive presence?"

He was right; the kitten was, in fact, gone. But it still seemed unsatisfactory to Amaand. "I just don't see why all this was necessary. I mean, I overdosed on expired pills!"

"And that's why you are my favorite daughter-in-law."

"There had to be a better way," she insisted.

His eyes widened as he considered her statement. "Oh,

KITTEN

I'm quite sure there was, definitely," he assented.

"What about me? Am I your favorite, too?" Trevor shrilled.

"And you are my favorite... grandson."

It was a very touching moment, disrupted abruptly when the phone rang.

"Hello?" Amaand answered.

"It's me again," said Ted.

"Yeah."

"I just wanted to make sure you guys were okay and the kitten was gone."

"Yeah, we're fine. Kitten is nowhere to be seen. I guess you and Marvin really pulled it off, huh?"

"Don't underestimate yourself. You did a lot today, and I'm proud to have you as my, uh, ex-wife. Just let Trevor know that I love him. I really enjoyed our time together. I'm sorry I'm insane. Take care. And be nicer to Trevor."

"And Ted... I want you to know that I... I don't hate you."

"Thanks, that means a lot right now." *Click.*

Marvin gathered his things, kissed Trevor on the head and left. The dead girl returned to the trunk. Amaand got Trevor ready for bed. It was nearly nine o'clock.

CHAPTER EIGHT

"Mommy, before you tuck me in, can you read me my favorite story? Please, please, please?"

She felt that Trevor deserved it after almost being eaten by the strange man who now lay dead upon her family room floor, surrounded by his own vomit stains. "Okay, honey." She grabbed the golden-bound book entitled *Pee Baby* and opened it to page three, where the story began. "Once upon a time," she read, "there were a boy and girl who were friends. They played together all day. They also drank a lot of apple juice. Then the girl said, 'I have to go take a pee.' She went and took a pee. After she was done the boy said, 'Now I have to pee, too.' He went and took a pee. And as he finished the little girl called to him, 'Oh no! I forgot to flush! I hope you didn't pee yet.' The little boy said, 'I did pee. I'm all done.' The little girl said, 'We might make a pee baby if you peed on top of my pee. Look and see.' And when the little boy looked in the toilet bowl, he saw a pee baby there. 'I'm going to try to flush it,' the boy said. But the baby was too big to go down. The little girl came in and pulled the baby out of the toilet and wrapped him in a towel. 'You are going to have to get a job,' she said to the boy. The next day he went and got a job in the salt mines. He worked very hard and every night he came home to the little girl and the pee baby and he asked the girl how the day was and she would say, 'It's so hard to be a little girl raising a pee baby.' 'I love you,' said the little boy. The pee baby cried and smelled a lot. The little boy worked and worked, all the while saving up

KITTEN

his money. One day after work the little boy stopped by the store and bought a blender. He took it home and he and the girl put the pee baby in the blender on puree. Then they could flush it neatly down the toilet. The end." The pictures were very well drawn, though the last picture was a bit troubling and almost got the book banned in those states that still try to ban books.

Amaand looked down at Trevor, whose eyes were closed peacefully, and saw a sweet angel of a boy. That was the way she wanted to see him every day. She kissed his forehead. "Good night, sweetheart." And she went to her own bedroom, where she promptly collapsed on her bed. She pulled off her shoes and tossed them. They fell haphazardly into opposite corners. Scrunching up her face, she tried to connect Marvin, the dead girl, the Collector, the kitten and Ted in a meaningful mental flowchart.

And she'd almost done it when Trevor burst into her room screaming, "I'm a kitten, Mommy!" He was covered in stamps. Apparently, his idea of a joke.

"Trevor! It's bed time, so get back in there and don't make me tan your hide!" She realized this was the worst form of parenting ever invented—constantly threatening the child with physical violence and then never delivering punishment of any kind—but it was also one of the easiest forms of parenting to use when she was exhausted from a day of adventure.

She shooed him into his bedroom, tutting down his protests and assuring him he would be tired if he just lay down and closed his eyes. She tucked him in again, turned out the light, and then stood in the doorway for several minutes until she could hear his breathing pattern change. She closed the bedroom door, yawned and shook her head, and then turned on the spectral gate over Trevor's doorway just to be sure of a good night's sleep.

PART TWO:

THE REVENGE

CHAPTER ONE

The kitten was walking, already in motion, when he became aware of his new surroundings. The sky in this place was dark, with only a dim reddish glow on the horizon. His paws chilled on contact with the ground, apparently made of steel, as if he was on some gigantic satellite. But the surface was not smooth and seemed to be less intentionally designed than the result of some colossal preternatural process. Never previously one to ponder such things, the kitten was surprised by his own thoughts about the nature of the world. He took note of the sparse, twisted vegetation that sprang forth from the hard, metallic earth: bare trees and cartoonish thorn brambles.

Then something else caught his eye—his own paw. It was not as he remembered it, but was now that of an orange tabby cat. He was no longer a kitten who was not a kitten; he was a kitten who was a kitten. Just as the realization dawned on him, he was hauled up into the air. Frantically, he flailed his limbs, but they caught on cords, a web, a net of some kind. Snared, dangling ten feet off the ground. The red of the sky had dimmed to a deep purple. Night was coming and there was no telling how long he might be trapped.

The night sky was full of royal blue stars. A sound like grinding gears would occasionally spring up, and a gurgling like a clogged drain seemed to draw nearer from behind him. Eventually, these sounds died out and the stars went black and there was nothing much to do. He felt truly alone for the first time. With no idea where he was,

G. Arthur Brown

no idea how far he was from the only people he knew, his loneliness gradually gave way to boredom. "I guess I'll just sing myself a song," he said. The only song he knew was *Lollipop* and singing that was not fun for him because he couldn't do the popping sound that makes the song so catchy. It was not too long before the kitten lost interest and fell asleep...

...Only to be jarred awake by the nipping of his fur by a small, moist mouth. In the dark it appeared to the kitten, surprised by just how good his night vision had become, that a fish had swum through the sky into the top of the net and was trying desperately to eat him. It came at him again, mouth agape, clamping its fishy jaws around his leg. Panicking, the kitten bit the fish right in the face. "Yow!" a voice outside the net said. Then the net was lowered to the ground and another fish entered. The two fish somehow scooped up the kitten and flew him to the ugly, bearded face of a 40-something man.

Lit by a nearby tiki torch, the man cocked his head and squinted at the kitten, as if blinded by the sheen of his fur. "You are not a gun," he said. "Why are you in my net? Why did you bite me?"

The kitten simply stared back at him.

"Answers, answers, answers!" shouted the man. "Answers are always necessary when questions are asked! Otherwise, why bother inventing questions in the first place!"

It occurred to the kitten that everyone he'd met so far had been a bit insane. He rolled his eyes, sighed, and said, "I guess this guy is crazy, too."

Hurt, the man pulled back his head. "What makes you say that? You are not a very nice kitten."

"You can hear me?"

"I certainly can! I have six sets of ears, two additional

KITTEN

on each of my fish-hands, so I can feel every ounce of that cat-venom you pack into your crude insults and accusations. It is not easy being different... having fish for hands! Sure, it is hard to pick things up. I lack manual dexterity, but that is just the tip of the molehill! I mean to say that people and cats like you go around judging me all the time." He pointed a fish accusatorily at the kitten. "Judger!"

"These fish are your hands?" the kitten asked in a tone he hoped indicated passivity, but it was the first day with his new vocal cords.

The man evidently took it as further derision. "Of course these fish are my hands! What do you think, you stupid cat? That two flying fish came and pulled you out of the net? Do you think I have trained sea creatures that do my bidding and bring the kittens I accidently catch in my gun traps to me for interrogation? Perhaps they put on a fanciful aquacade to appease me, for I must be a cruel..." he looked into the kitten's eyes with spite, "...and crazy taskmaster."

"Calm down," said the kitten. "I'm not trying to insult you. I'm just trying to make sense of things. I've never been to a place where the ground is metal and I've never met a man with fish for hands. This world is strange to me. I'm not really sure how I even got here. Or why I can speak. So, if you'd just chill out and lay off me for a minute, I'd thank you."

The fish-handed man set the kitten on the ground. "Ah, I am sorry. I did not realize you were a newcomer." He placed his right fish over his heart. "I am called Tamanney. Come back to my hovel for a rest and something to eat, please." His fishy hands, now empty, stared blankly at the kitten and made kissy faces. A bite mark was visible on the right fish, bleeding a little. The man was dressed in black armor, crudely crafted from bits of the steel landscape. Matching black leather provided scant covering for his lower half.

Tamanney truly lived in a hovel; he wasn't just being humble. One wall was earthen, another corrugated aluminum overlapping an irregular sheet of plywood. The roof was thatched except where it was open to the sky. Plastic grocery bags with small holes poked in them covered windows cut in the walls. But Tamanney was gracious and hospitable, and despite his fish-hands, he managed to prepare a small meal for the kitten. He dropped pans and pots constantly and the fish faces stared as if in astonishment at what they'd done. But Tamanney didn't become angry. He simply picked up whatever he had dropped and went on, pretending nothing had happened. The meal was not what the kitten was expecting, consisting of the muzzle of an old flintlock and a few braised musket balls. He licked at the gravy that covered them, which turned out to be gun oil. Being extremely hungry, he took a bite. To the kitten's surprise, he managed to eat quite easily and found the taste peculiar but not unpleasant.

"What is this place?" he asked between mouthfuls.

"This is the world."

"Well, I was in a world before. What world is this one?"

"This is the world of the living. The Steel Planet. You must have been brought here from the world of the dead."

The kitten wasn't sure what Tamanney meant. "Why would I go from the world of the dead to the world of the living?"

"Where else does the Lord God get the parts to create new life? He must rob graves. Pull from the junk heaps to create new and wonderful things. Nothing comes from nothing."

KITTEN

Incredulous, the kitten added, "In the other world I was a kitten that was not a kitten."

"In the world of the dead all kittens are not kittens."

"That's not what I mean. Maybe in the world of the dead the kittens *are not*, but they are not *not kittens*, like I was."

"Oh! Double negative," Tamanney barked and pulled a card out of a pocket in his leggings. He gave this card to the kitten, who, having no hands, did not take the card but read it aloud:

"This is a warning issued by the Council of Lord God to any who utter the double negative. Collect three and be escorted immediately to the Room of Questions." He looked at Tamanney. "What does this mean?"

The man slapped a fish against his knee. "What does your double negative mean, I ask you? What does *anything* mean? We can ask that question all day, like drunken philosophers. But you have one card so you have been warned."

"Where am I supposed to keep the card? It's not like I've got pockets."

"Do not worry about that. It will keep *you*. But you are a newcomer. Many newcomers receive one card. It is not a big deal. The biggest deal right now, little kitten, is what is your name?"

The chirping of metallic insects in the alien night resounded as the kitten pondered. "I don't think I have one."

"No name? Had you no master?"

"I did have a master, a boy named Trevor, but he called me his kitten. He never gave me a name."

Tamanney, seeming alarmed, waved his fish about frantically. "All things must have names! Quickly then, we must give you a name!"

G. Arthur Brown

"Okay, give me one!" said the kitten to placate his exasperated host.

Putting one of his fish lips in his human mouth, Tamanney hummed. "Let's see. I think we should name you... Tamanney!"

The kitten giggled. "It would be confusing if we both had the name Tamanney, don't you think?"

"But my name is not Tamanney. That is only what I am called. My true name is kept secret in the soul of my heart."

"Still, if I am *named* Tamanney and you are *called* Tamanney, it will confuse people."

"What people are you speaking of?"

"Like if someone was to write a story about us, you know, in the future, and people read about us. They might have a hard time telling which is which."

"Maybe," Tamanney assented. He screwed up his face and looked at his feet. "I am just not very good with names."

"You must know more names than just Tamanney."

Tamanney nodded. "Oh, yes. I had almost forgotten. What about... Willoughby?"

The kitten felt suddenly warm inside when he considered the name. It brought a bit of a smile to his cat lips. "Yes, Willoughby would be just fine."

"Ha ha! Willoughby it is! Willoughby the kitten!"

Willoughby's warm fuzzies did not last long. With a loud clatter, a flaming arrow lodged itself in the wall next to Tamanney's head, juddering and producing an almost musical buzz. In the blink of an eye, Tamanney leapt up and back-flipped, narrowly avoiding another fiery missile headed right for his face. "What's going on?" hollered Willoughby. He turned around to see a man in black pushing away the window bag with the tip of an arrow.

KITTEN

A snap caught Willoughby's attention from a different window, where a young boy in black was taking photographs. A second snap as a harpoon split the boy's nose, and blood flowed forth as if Tamanney had used the spear to turn on a faucet. The boy fell lifelessly below the window and out of sight while the man with the bow withdrew, the sound of pounding feet disappearing into the distance.

Tamanney, gripping a second harpoon in a fish fist poised for action, smirked and said to Willoughby, "Neighbors."

CHAPTER TWO

Under a gray sky, Tamanney clumsily carried the body of the neighbor boy to a nearby ravine. After a quick check of the pockets, producing only a hardboiled lizard egg, the man kicked the body over the precipice, and Willoughby watched in awe as it tumbled ungracefully down the side of the crag to the jagged rock bed below.

"Lord God," said Tamanney plaintively, "we commit this corpse to the pit, that it may serve as fodder for the next world. Make him into a toy monkey that clashes together two tin cymbals unmusically, or, if you so see fit, turn his skin into a sort of leather to upholster the strange and wonderful furniture that the people of the next world lounge upon. I am sorry his family is not very good at killing me. I regret everything and nothing, all at once. Does this make me a bad man, Lord God?" He stared up into the hazy sky and yelped like a startled hound. Turning to Willoughby, he reiterated: "Does that make me a bad man, Willoughby?"

Willoughby did not understand the ways of this world and simply stated, "That's a question every cat must answer for himself."

"I will not let this ruin my day," the fish-handed man said, rubbing scaly flesh against his eyes to wipe the tears away, which only served to redden the eyelids even further. "I will save the film from his camera and we'll develop it in the Town today. What do you think of a little trip into town, Willoughby? Ready for high adventure?"

KITTEN

"Sounds heart-stopping," said the kitten with something less than full conviction.

"You might," said Tamanney, bashfully, "be able to find a job while we are there. If you were thinking of looking for one."

It had never occurred to Willoughby that kittens might be able to procure jobs for themselves. He suddenly felt a sort of existential crisis descend upon him. If he was now a free kitten, with no master, he would be required to look after himself, and as such, he would need a plan for the future. A reason for existence. "Wow, yeah. I'll look into that, I guess. What am I going to do with my life?"

The two caught sight of a young, curly-headed blonde boy in a blue suit of clothes. "Hello! Hello, I say!" The boy waved at them wildly. "I have come to this Steel Planet all the way from a private world, B-612, where only I live, alone. I flew here using birds to meet other individuals and discover the point of existence. Could you draw me a picture of a kitten that is not a kitten?"

"I'm sorry," Willoughby said bluntly, "but I really don't have time for you right now." The boy blushed and turned away, finding the nearest ugly shrub to examine and fall in love with. Tamanney ate the lizard egg he had found in the corpse's pocket, and the two set about making preparations to go to the Town.

CHAPTER THREE

Tamanney owned a tired old donkey with velveteen hide that tottered forward slightly faster than a decaying terrapin. On the poor creature's back, the pair made their way to the Town under an oppressive, steely sun. A worn bridle was clenched in fishy mouths while flies gathered and buzzed, as they might around the head of a smelly boy in a park. Willoughby, perched atop the man's left shoulder, felt the breeze—what little there was of it—against his furry face. "I'm the king of the world!" he said playfully.

"Shhhh!" chided Tamanney. "You do not wish the Lord God to hear you, do you? What would he say to your words? He would tell you that *he* is the king of the world and he might take away your collectibles. Lock you in a safe deposit box. Or worse." With a grimace: "He might sell you on eBay."

The little donkey trudged down an escarpment, inch by inch, a few feet an hour it seemed, until they came to a rusty valley filled with trees—or something very much like them—made of glued-together popsicle sticks. A few small pistols skittered about like prairie dogs. One stopped and appeared to stare at the travelers.

"Ooh, look!" said Willoughby.

"Pshht. Glocks," said Tamanney dismissively. As if emotionally hurt, the small guns scuttled down into a burrow and out of sight. There was nothing much left to look at, except the grim sky. But a sudden roaring below grabbed the kitten's attention. It echoed from the distance, over rusty knolls.

KITTEN

"W-what was that?"

Tamanney reached a fish hand into his satchel. "Giant pandas." He pulled out some feathers and plastic beads, then started to fix them all around the kitten.

"W-what are you doing?"

"I am disguising us as a fashionable hat," the man said impatiently. "This is mating season, so the giant pandas will be migrating south, right in the direction of the Town. If we can convince them we are a fashionable hat, one might put us on and we can hitch a much faster ride than the donkey can give us." Then, patting the donkey's head, he said, "Sorry, girl. Or boy. I can never remember which." He tied some sparkly glass beads into the mane.

"Aren't we all a bit too big to fit on a panda's head?"

"*Giant* panda," Tamanney corrected. He tied a gold scarf on his head. "Now be perfectly still and try to look as much like a fashionable hat as you can."

From behind one of the knolls, a head emerged. When the beast reared itself up on its hind legs it stood over three stories tall—a true giant panda. Willoughby hoped it was more in the mood for a hat than for food. Striding majestically across the barren earth, the panda headed directly toward them. It stopped a few yards away and considered them with sidelong glances. Then it said something very enthusiastically in panda language, reached out a paw to pick them up and placed them on its head. They were exactly the panda's size and fashionable enough to suit its taste.

"Getting off near the Town might be a bit tricky," Tamanney whispered.

The panda continued on its way south, occasionally roaring and adjusting its new fashionable hat. Before long, it met another even more gigantic panda, which was clearly envious of the fashionable hat. They chatted in panda language, and Willoughby swore he saw understanding of the words in the donkey's eyes, though the tongue is certainly unknown to men and kittens. The conversation lasted what seemed to Willoughby to be an eternity. The beasts said their goodbyes and then they were off again, still heading southerly.

After about an hour, they came to a dale where a collection of wooden shacks, block tenements, tin storehouses and stone spires jutted forth from the cracked, harsh landscape. A bloody smell filled the air. Tamanney sighed and whispered, "The Town. You will never find a more wretched hive of junk and miscellany. We must be cautious." But the kitten was more concerned about how they would get off the panda's head. In a bizarre twist of fate, however, the panda bartered them to a fashionable hat trader who had a small post right outside the Town. It set them down and wandered off with a new mood ring on its paw.

The fashionable hat trader was an older woman wearing dark sunglasses and a loud Acapulco shirt that was unbuttoned quite low, revealing most of her sagging, rumpled breasts. She eyed the group up.

"As you can see, madam," Tamanney said, "we are not actually a fashionable hat."

"Ain't a fashionable hat, eh? I bought ya so I'm a put ya'll in my store shed." She tried to lift the donkey, struggling for a few seconds before giving up.

"I'm very sorry about your mood ring," Willoughby said.

"No fashionable hat tells me it's sorry and gets away with it!" She rattled her fist, smacked her lips and shook her head. Then she pulled a coupon out of her pocket and began reading it. Tamanney urged the donkey on as the trader grumbled loudly about expiration dates.

CHAPTER FOUR

They entered by the east gate, above which hung a sign that read "The Town of the Town." The words "Welcome to" had obviously been painted over. A man dressed a little too much like the Jack of Diamonds stood watch, eyed the two warily, but waved them through without any questions. The streets were unpaved except with filth and trash. The tinny sound of a small musical ensemble filled the air. The tune was *The Theme from the Greatest American Hero*, which Willoughby thought he recognized but couldn't quite place. Out of the bustling crowd of peasants, a curly-headed blonde man in a red suit approached and said, "Hello! I was sent to this world from my home planet to fight crime and defend the innocent. I'm not quite sure how my powers work, because I lost the manual for this suit. Anybody could have been a hero in my place. Generally, I bumble my way through to success. Do you know of any wrongs that need righting?"

Tamanney held up a fish. "We do not want what you are selling, Earthling."

"I'm not selling anything. I was just hoping you could tell me—"

"I'm sorry, but I don't have time for you right now," Willoughby said, and the two plodded forward, still on donkeyback, meandering their way through the smelly, odd crowd. Emerging briefly from the mob, an orphan boy threw a severed finger at Tamanney. It ricocheted off his head and hit Willoughby. "Fuck that kid!" the kitten spat.

Tamanney turned and shouted after the boy, "Whose

finger was that?" He righted himself and quietly lamented: "I'll never have fingers of my very own."

Willoughby felt a need to say something conciliatory. "Aw, you don't need hands, Tamanney."

"But I *want* hands," he pouted.

"Having fish for hands is what makes you unique, you know? If you didn't have fish for hands you'd be just like those freaks who have been hounding us all day. I saw the way you hurled that harpoon into the neighbor boy. You don't need hands, my friend. Trust me."

Tamanney smiled, a flicker in his weary eyes. Then he frowned again. "But I *want* hands!"

On the street corner ahead, a long-haired messiah was preaching behind a flaming barrel and holding up a model airplane with its belly forward and nose up, forming roughly the shape of a cross. "One Friday morning, late on a Wednesday night, I was on both sides of the world at once! Airfare is a conspiracy, my friends. Travelling around the skies in a huge arc, bah! I have a plane that goes straight through the *soul*!" Then a little capuchin monkey dressed as a flight steward popped out from behind the messiah's legs and started collecting the luggage of the gathered followers.

"Look how strong that monkey is," Willoughby said. The small simian heaped at least twenty bags, each twice the primate's size, on its shoulders.

"Or how light the luggage is," Tamanney added with a wink. "The faithful always travel light." The two moved on.

Straight ahead, standing thirty feet tall, was a hulking statue, the sight of which instantly chilled Willoughby right through his fur to the bone. It was of a man with a fat belly, gaunt face and coke bottle glasses. A Panama hat sat atop the head. "What the hell is that statue doing here?" he asked, a slight quaver in his voice.

KITTEN

"That is one of the many monuments to the Lord God you will find on the Steel Planet. The Town is quite a devout place. You will find very few heretics here. And if you do find any, please alert one of the Jacks."

"That... that is the man who killed me. He ate me whole!"

"You mean you have met him? Quickly, let us shake hands." The fact that neither had hands didn't stop Tamanney from enveloping the kitten's forepaw in the mouth of a fish and frantically pumping it up and down. "Few are brought to the world by the Lord God personally. Many come here by flames." Willoughy was too vexed to continue speaking, so he licked himself all over and tried to hide his shaking.

Tamanney dismounted, Willoughby still on his shoulder, and found a hostler to keep his donkey.

CHAPTER FIVE

Tamanney and a short, plump, bald woman with no neck haggled in a foreign tongue amid the open-air market. The sounds of the words brought forth spittle from Tamanney's mouth and small sand-crab-like creatures from the woman's. Their voices grew louder and more guttural, hands waved about; small items were dashed against the ground. Willoughby gathered that they could not agree on a reasonable price for photo developing.

A woman's voice, like a sultry female Dracula, spoke into Willoughby's left ear: "Hey there, little one. Do you look for sex with me?"

Willoughby turned to find the source of the voice: a five-foot woman in a red felt suit ostensibly designed to look like a cat. She removed a large, round cathead to reveal a face painted up like a clown's, but with whiskers drawn on the cheeks. "I make the sex with cats for football cards or costume jewelry. But only jewelry with red stones to match my dress." Her dress, presumably, was her cat costume.

"Lady, I have other things on my mind right now."

"I can make it so nothing on mind, only on wiener."

"What... did... you... just... say?" said Willoughby breathlessly.

"I don't mind the barbs of the cat penis."

"Leave me alone," the kitten said and shuddered.

"What? You go and call the Jacks on me, little cat?" Willoughby said nothing.

"You come find Nanarina when you ready to stop

playing dumb, ready to start playing sex." She brushed his chin with the tip of her finger and prowled away, in the very poorest imitation of a cat Willoughby had ever seen.

Willoughby shook, fumed. He whispered into Tamanney's ear, "Get me out of this crazy place."

"Shhh! I almost have her down to a dagger with a goat-foot handle and three conch shells with names of Caribbean islands printed on them."

Eventually, an agreement was made, though Tamanney seemed less than pleased about the price. While they waited for the photos to be developed, they ducked into a small, salt-aired tavern that served something it called ice cream, but which was, in fact, bland, flash-frozen dots. Tamanney ate from a small cup with a tiny plastic spoon clenched in fishy lips and squealed, "This is how you know you are in the future!" He grinned insanely and even let Willoughby eat off the same spoon.

"If we are in the future, why did we just ride a donkey?"

"Cat, you are too cynical. Do you know how long it took our scientist to invent the donkey? The research was quite expensive, I can tell you."

"Scientist? You mean there's only one on the Steel Planet?"

Tamanney lowered his brow and scoffed. "How many do you need on your world? One is more than enough."

"I don't actually know how many there are on my world, but it must be thousands at least."

"And where do you get enough virgins to pay them with?"

"I suspect most of them are paid in cash."

"What is this *cash*?"

"Currency... money."

Tamanney's blank face showed no sign of recognition.

"Look," continued Willoughby, "it's really not important. But, uh, do you really pay your scientist in virgins?"

"Yes, yes. We cook the virgins first, of course."

Willoughby shuddered at the thought, but he had bigger fish to fry, and not his friend's hands, either. Namely, there was the Collector, the Lord God of the Steel Planet, who had brought him here, but he also had his agents in the other world. One name specifically was seared into his mind: Amaand. She had summoned the Collector, the kitten knew this much. A purpose for his existence was forming. He wanted revenge. On the softer side of his mind he had fond memories of the boy, Trevor, the one who had loved him. He could not leave the boy in the care of such a wicked woman who was supposed to be mothering him. It was unthinkable. He wanted to put things right.

"Tamanney, do you know of any way I could get back to the world I came from?"

CHAPTER SIX

The pictures came out great. "This is my favorite attempt on my life," Tamanney confessed, delicately using his fish to flip through the prints to minimize the slimy stains left on their surfaces. "Look at this one! See how close that arrow was to my head!"

"I don't understand why your neighbors were trying to kill you."

"I am their neighbor, Willoughby. Is that not enough?"

"The boy really was an exceptional photographer," Willoughby conceded.

"I know. It breaks my heart that his father was not better with the bow. The photographs of my murder would have been some of the most spectacular of all time, suitable for a museum exhibition. My lifeless corpse slowly being engulfed in flames, the inferno of my hovel around me as I am reduced to ashes that blow triumphantly into the next world. I only hope they would have done me the honor of tossing whatever bits of me were left into some ravine."

The sun was about to set. "We must get lodgings here for tonight," the man told the kitten, "but we can set out at first light for the Children's Isle to see what we can do to get you back to your world. That is, if I am not killed tonight by any of my neighbors who might have followed us into town."

Ultimately, their room proved as uninviting as Tamanney's hovel, though the roach infestation entertained Willoughby for quite a while until he was tired enough to fall asleep on the faux-wood floor.

CHAPTER SEVEN

The soft touch of a feminine hand upon his whiskers roused Willoughby from his slumber. In the dark, he was just able to discern a medium-sized human silhouette, but with pointed feline ears. "We now sex, little kitty; we now sex," said the female voice. "Nanarina always know how to sex you right. I do for free, little kitty. Don't worry." She grabbed Willoughby and began to pull him toward her crotch while he desperately thrashed about, hoping to sink his claws into whatever he could. "Why you shy? You no like Nanarina?" He could feel his head being enveloped in a fleshy cavern.

A scream woke him. It was his own. "Just a dream," he panted. Tamanney, unfazed, snored softly. Then the kitten noticed a medium-sized human form, but this was not a silhouette. It was a teenage boy glowing with a soft, angelic light. From a bookshelf in the room he selected books and then rearranged them all alphabetically by title. He smelled familiar to Willoughby, and looked like an older version of Trevor, roaming somnolently and muttering, "I miss my kitten."

"Trevor?" Willoughby said quietly. The apparition stopped for a moment as if listening, then proceeded to pace and mumble. "Trevor!" the kitten said more loudly.

This time the boy looked at Willoughby and approached. "What are you doing in my dreams, kitten? You don't look like I remember." He leaned forward and picked Willoughby up and petted him absently. "You feel like a different kitten."

KITTEN

"Trevor, it *is* me! I'm your kitten, but now I'm a real kitten. I was sent to this strange place by the Collector. I'm going to find a way back to you, to save you from your mother."

The boy's face crept toward a grin, but then fell blank again. "You haunt me. When I awake this memory will cause me pain. I shall not remember this," Trevor said flatly.

"No! Listen to me; you must remember! We are really here together on the Steel Planet. Your astral body has somehow projected itself here, seeking me maybe, while you sleep. Tell your mother that she had better make things right. But this is not just a dream! You must remember. You must!"

Trevor's attention had wandered. "I wonder what episode of *Pirate Piet* will be on today. Will it be the one where he says he loves me?" The boy set the kitten on the floor, but a quick strike of the claws caught his hand before he could pull away. "Yow! Meanie!" He was more alert now.

"Now that I've got your attention, be expecting my return. I'm trapped for now, but I'm coming back to your world. When I get there some changes will take place, oh you bet!"

"Am I in the future?" Trevor asked, eying his own spectral, teenage figure.

"Well, I did have some frozen dots that were simply called 'ice cream.' I think the timelines of the worlds must not line up exactly. Your spirit isn't the same age as your body, maybe. Or the astral plane could be timeless."

"Sounds like you are pulling that out of your butt, kitten. I want orange juice…"

"Call me Willoughby. I have a name now."

The boy was already fading away into nothingness, returning to his own space and time. Willoughby could only hope that the boy would remember something. And he clung urgently to the notion that he would find a way back to Trevor, a way back home.

CHAPTER EIGHT

Willoughby awoke the next morning already aboard a boat. Tamanney had kindly carried him without waking him up. Looking out a grimy porthole, the kitten saw cloudy brown water where it met the rusty shoreline. It was a steam-powered vessel they traveled on, an antique that had seen better days. "We are on the canal that leads to the loch in which sits the Children's Isle," Tamanney told him. "We will be there before evening. I suspect the King of Children can instruct us on how to get you home, little friend."

Willoughby smiled a kitten smile. "Thank you for helping me. I'd be lost without you."

"It is I who should be thanking you," countered Tamanney.

"Really? Why is that?"

"Until you came, my life was sorrowfully empty but for the continued thwarting of my neighbors' attempts to murder me horribly. It is now as if I have a purpose, even if that purpose will vanish with you." Willoughby thought this sounded melodramatic. Nonetheless, it made him feel good about himself.

Capt. Swann, the grizzled seadog and only other person aboard the boat, staggered his way into their shoddy quarters with a cup of grog in one hand and singing, "De auld Maid of Spain, she were made outta pain. And the staples what fastened her together, bits of turtle-hide leather. She had no disease when upon the High Seas, but the men who fill her belly, often drink napalm jelly..."

KITTEN

The tune was something the old man had heard on a *Power Ballads of the Cold War* commercial. "Awake now, are we?" he said to Willoughby, and then laughed so hard that the rotting stench of his gums filled the cabin.

"Is the passage a dangerous one, Captain?" asked Tamanney.

"What?" said Willoughby. "You are just now asking this? That would be the first thing I'd ask before chartering the boat!"

Tamanney looked embarrassed and ran a fish over his beard nervously.

"Belay your fears, boys. The passage ain't dangerous. Naw, nothing to her. We'll set in as easy as a hoisted Horace Johnson into the porthole of a powder monkey." Capt. Swann took another swig of his liquor and then reflected, "Though, some a them powder monkeys can put up a fight, nows I think about it. Lost my big toe and my left ball to one, sorry to say."

"What's he talking about?" Willoughby asked.

Tamanney merely shook his head discouragingly and changed the subject. "I have heard tales of the sirens frequenting the shallows here in Aichenarb Loch. Their songs are said to be so beautiful that sailors think they are about to be arrested."

"The music may be as beautiful as all that," said Capt. Swann, "but it'll be the last thing ya hears, no doubt about it. Anyway, sirens is all a bunch of hokum like mermaids and watermelons. No melons grow in the seas! Just a story to scare the lily-livered away to lub on land."

The captain proved to be very knowledgeable about the sea and all its lore. He told Willoughby the story of Dr. Jesu's Cabinet, in which the souls of Jewish sailors drowned at sea are stuffed until such time as their families can ransom them with golden chicken bouillon. He spoke also of times before the canal when the Town was completely landlocked and they couldn't get imported goods like oranges or lapels. Willoughby grew fond of the captain and trusted him almost completely. Tamanney, on the other hand, grew wary and standoffish, and went above decks for some air.

"I don't think your friend likes me very much," said Capt. Swann.

"He has a hard time getting along with most people, including his neighbors." Willoughby noticed a green, smeary mark on the old man's forearm. "What's that tattoo of, Captain?"

A wistful reverie took Capt. Swann and he sat down on a dusty steamer trunk. He looked cautiously at his own arm, as if trying not to spook it. "That... I haven't thought of that in many a year."

The kitten, quietly but assuringly said, "Tell me the story."

The man breathed heavily, and it appeared to Willoughby there was a tear in the corner of his eye. "Some things... better left forgotten. But, if you must know, the tattoo was a kind of goblin, a booger more like, with a face and arms, holding a spear. A picture that I found on the wall of a tattoo parlor. I had clams in me pocket just a burning a hole right through, so I picked it on a whim. Regretted it ever since. This was in my youth, a lad of sixteen. Back on Earth, mind you. Before I came here to Limbo."

The kitten was surprised. "Tamanney said that this was the world of the living; that Earth was the world of the dead."

"Your friend is as much a fool as he is an inflamed barnacle. Sure, there's some what'll tell ya this world is the world of the living. There's some says we're in Hell now. And yet others, bat-shit crazy though they be, say this here is Paradise. But my theory is, and I've heard it said by learned men too, that we are in Limbo, waiting to move on to higher or lower realms." The man looked up and down respectively as he spoke.

Willoughby's excitement mounted. "Is it possible, do you know, to return to my world?"

The captain rubbed his bushy brow. "There are certain gateways, if you are looking for them. Most are the sort a man never wants to have to cross, though. I've heard it said by many a learned man, and even more not-so-learned ones, that the gateway to this world we are in lies chiefly in the belly of the compulsively gathering demiurge—Lord God as he calls himself. The gateway out of this world then is said to be a spewing out by his opposite, an eschewing rascal by the name of the Chunder Lord. It is him, they say, what spits you back onto the shores whence you come."

"Do you believe these stories?" asked the kitten.

"It ain't so much a matter if I believe or don't. It's a matter of what other option ya got. Ain't so you can just waltz through a door and find yourself home, I shouldn't think. This here be the only way I've heard. For better or worse, you go with what you know."

"How can I find the Chunder Lord?"

"Alas, the tricky part." He rubbed his scraggly chin and shook his head. "I used to have a card with an address and his office hours, but I lost it long ago to the maw of a saltwater crocodile. As to where this Chunder Lord may be, your guess is as good as mine. Though it looks like your friend thinks the King of Children may have some information about the matter. And for what I know, he may. But I'll tell you that the Children's Isle is as close a place to Hell as I've ever seen and I don't ever wish to set foot back there. The King is mad and so is his witch. That island is a refuge for juvenile delinquents and runaways. Well, I say refuge, but it is also a cage."

"So, the dock is the end of the line for you?" Willoughby asked with a lilting of sadness.

"Aye, my little kitten friend. Aye."

Tamanney called from above decks, "Land ho, Captain!" Swann patted the kitten's head and gave a nod before returning to the helm.

CHAPTER NINE

Children's Isle appeared to be a normal tropical island like the ones on Earth. From the docks, Willoughby saw white sand beaches, palm trees, bright flowers and foliage, and an array of colorful parrots. "This doesn't look like such a bad place," he said to Swann.

"Notice how there are no humans around," Tamanney said. He held a fish up over his eyes to shield them from the bright afternoon sun. "Where are all the children?"

"Hiding in their devil pits," barked Swann as he rummaged through a crate. He pulled out a small bundle of dynamite and handed it to Tamanney, who clumsily took it between both his fish hands and slid it into his satchel. "They go invisible when they are watching."

"I see one now," said Willoughby. On the beach there was a lone boy with curly blonde locks, dressed in a grass skirt and shell necklace.

"Ahoy there!" called the boy. "I've been shipwrecked here with just one other girl. We know little of the world and are discovering our bodies together. Could you help us, please?"

"I'm sorry," Willoughby said flatly. "We really don't have time for your crap, kid. I'm out for revenge."

The boy sank in disappointment and kicked a shell.

Swann raised an eyebrow. "None of the little buggers afoot. I smell something fishy, and it ain't your friend's hands," he said to Willoughby. Willoughby wondered if it could be the man's own clothes that had no doubt been worn for at least a month at sea.

"Ambush?" Tamanney asked.

Willoughby trembled. "I've got a bad feeling about this."

Swann grabbed a shotgun from his gun cabinet. "Looks like I'll be coming along after all." Willoughby felt slightly better upon hearing this, though Tamanney pulled a snide face. The old captain smiled crudely. "Can't leave you alone with this fish-handed freak, Willoughby."

Tamanney groaned. "I will have you know, Capt. Swann, that I am perfectly capable of killing children."

"Sure and I don't doubt it. One at a time, though. Ever taken on a whole platoon of them?"

Tamanney was about to fire back when Willoughby interrupted: "Gentlemen, let's not bicker. You are both fully capable murderers. What we need now is some kind of plan."

"Let me think of what I recall of this here island," Swann said, scratching his chin with his shotgun. As he mulled it over, Willoughby's gaze once again returned to the lone child on the beach. The boy was collecting seaweed, furtively glancing at the boat every few seconds. Willoughby was just beginning to suspect he was up to something when a primitive spear punctured the boy's back and sent him toppling into the surf. A group of small figures was now visible along the tree line.

"Great," said Swann. "The welcoming committee is here."

"Did you come up with a plan yet?" asked Tamanney. Swann scowled back and tucked a fistful of shells into his pocket.

A girl of about six sauntered toward the dock. She carried a spear almost twice her height. A blue velour robe swathed her form, and a cute cowgirl hat rested atop her amateur French braid. With lips smeared by improper lipstick application she said, "Hello. I am Nungnung, the ambassinator for visitors. I welcome you to Children's Isle. What's your beeswax here?"

Swann hesitated, so Tamanney spoke up: "We three seek the counsel of the King himself. Could you take us to him?"

"The King is busy. He's watching *Hankel and Schlege*. It don't go off till five. You wanna wait?"

Hankel and Schlege was a very popular sketch comedy show on the Steel Planet. The lead cast and writers, the eponymous Hankel and Schlege, had come from Vaudeville and dada cabaret respectively, so their humor had a bizarre but campy feel that appealed broadly to the lowest common denominator of that world.

"Oh! Can we watch it with him?" asked Tamanney, who was rather a big fan of the show.

She nodded. "You can watch in the Common Hall. If we go fast, you can prolly see the last part of it. Come on."

Tamanney grinned like a goon and rubbed his fish together. "It is an all-new episode tonight!"

Swann nudged him with the butt of his gun. "Don't get too comfy just yet, boy-o."

Tamanney stopped smiling and cleared his throat. "Right, right indeed." He snatched up Willoughby and set him on his shoulder.

CHAPTER TEN

A troupe of about a dozen children between the ages of five and eleven escorted the two men and the kitten along a sandy jungle path to the palace. Most of the boys were dressed in outfits reminiscent of 1960s Star Trek, though grungy and threadbare. The girls wore what their mothers would never let them: trampy make-up and oversized negligees. All carried spears with bamboo hafts—all except the one who had killed the blonde boy on the beach. That kid simply jumped around like a coked-up monkey and made armpit farts at the three visitors. As they walked, the children chanted, "Left. Left. Left, right, left," though they were not in any formation and none of their feet ever matched the orders spoken.

Willoughby noticed something strange about one of the girls. Something was wagging beneath her slip. "Holy shit. Look at the tail on her," he whispered to Tamanney.

The man shrugged. "She is too young for my taste."

"No, that's not what I—" but Willoughby cut himself short when the palace came into view. *Palace* may not be the best word to describe the building. It was half kid-fort made of sheets stretched over chairs and cushions, half old-Spanish mission with bell tower jutting out of the center of the complex, terra cotta tiled roof. A guard of kids patrolled outside the bedspread walls.

"I'd really feel better if you had a gun, too," Willoughby told Tamanney.

KITTEN

"I *am* quite famished. I have not eaten since last night," the man admitted.

"Enough with the witty banter," Swann broke in. "We need to keep our wits about us if we are going to survive this ordeal, I tell ya."

"How can we both end the witty banter and keep our wits?" asked Tamanney, who was never very good at jokes. The old captain just looked at him with the scorn that usually only a mother gives.

"Are we finished now, boys?" Swann pointed to the front gate. "Once we are in there, there's no way out. I'll have ya know that I ate a lot of spicy food last night, so if you smell something funny, it's probably coming from me. Don't worry about gas attacks. I doubt they got the technology. Worry about one of these delinquents shoving a spear tip in your ass, instead. They think it's very funny to do that, and if I'm honest, it *is* funny to watch. Not as funny to receive a stick in the bum, though. That's why I had all those videos of the powder monkeys… they make me laugh. Aye, they're funny. That's—"

Willoughby interrupted. "Capt. Swann. You led us to believe you had a plan of some kind?"

"Aye, little kitten, me mate, I do. Like I said, once inside, there's no turning back. So I suggest you go ahead and ask the King of Children your questions."

Both the kitten and the man with fish for hands stared silently.

The old man grinned and nodded. "Aye, boys. That's the plan."

"That is not a fucking plan!" screamed Willoughby.

A spear-bearing boy nearby shouted to the others, "The kitten and the old fart are gonna fight!"

"Ooh!" yelled the largest boy. Most of the others turned and laughed, while the one continued hopping and armpit-farting. A girl looked concerned. Maybe she loved kittens, as many little girls are wont to do, and was worried about his chances.

"There isn't going to be any fight!" said Willoughby. The captain and Tamanney both nodded in agreement. "It's just a misunderstanding."

"You know how I fix misunderstanding?" the largest boy said, a boy of about ten with spiky hair and bug-eyes. "Wif a trip to the Rena of Sport!"

Tamanney stared at his fish-hands and muttered, "This doesn't sound good."

"Rena! Rena!" the rest of the kids chanted, except for the armpit-farter who yelled, "Sport!" and made a few more fart noises. And they all ran off to the east, toward a small stadium, leaving the three visitors behind.

"What the fuck is going on here, Capt. Swann?" demanded Willoughby.

"How in the name of the Holy Mother of Retards should I know? This ain't the sea, kitten boy. You're on dry land, now."

Something had to be done. The kitten thought for a minute. "Okay. I've got an idea. Forming in my head…"

CHAPTER ELEVEN

The two guardsmen, young boys with machetes standing watch, were busy shouting profanity at each other when the three approached.

"What the bitch do you shitters want?" asked the freckly one on the right.

"Eat turds, crap heads! Go smoke some crap!" yelled the other, holding up his ring finger and sticking out his tongue.

"We just want to go in and ask the King a few questions," Willoughby said.

"Piss Puss! Pissy kitty pants!"

"Is that a no?"

"What do I look like," the freckly kid said, "the boss of you? Leave us alone, twat neck. We are busy guarding."

"Get out of our hair, hair rapers! Go rape your ears, you dumb fuckshits!"

"I'm glad I never had children," Swann said as they entered the gates to the palace. The interior left Willoughby feeling like the toddlers had definitely taken over the nursery. Every inch of wall had been drawn on in crayon, and it was evident that in some parts previous layers of crayon had been scraped off to make way for finger paints. They walked along a long corridor full of abandoned Johnny Jump Ups. Following it to the source of the laughter of a great many children, they found themselves in the Common Hall. They sat in folding chairs among the huge mass of snot-nosed sprogs who ogled the large movie screen with a mixture of awe and irreverence that only sugar-fueled sprats can muster.

G. Arthur Brown

"Hurray! We are not too late," said Tamanney, eyes fixed on the latest episode of *Hankel and Schlege*. Willoughby struggled to get a grasp on the current sketch, already in progress. A man dressed as a nun was playing a ukulele as a man in a bowler hat shook his fist from a nearby VW Beetle and shouted, "Go on up! Go up, thou bald head, go up!" The nun-man refused to move out of the way of the vehicle and, instead, began to sing, "Sometimes a guitar is too large when you just want a little ditty." But the driver of the car, rather comically enraged at this point with steam coming from his ears and green goo coming from his eyes, got out of the Bug, grabbed his umbrella and used it to whack the ukulele to the ground. When the nun rushed to snatch it back up, still singing, the man poked both his/her hands with the sharp tip of the umbrella. "Oh, for the sake of holy stigmata!" shouted the man-nun, holding up her/his palms to display holes right through them. Then the driver in the hat ripped off the nun's habit, revealing she was really a bald man (which anyone watching already knew) in a monk's habit. And the monk proceeded to go up, as instructed earlier. The entire audience was in stitches.

"Uh, what's going on?" Willoughby asked Tamanney.

"Schlege is the one in the bowler," he said, and then guffawed, perhaps embarrassingly if everyone else hadn't been doing the exact thing at the time. This explained nothing to the kitten, but a new sketch was starting, so he hoped maybe he would be able to follow this one a little better.

A man in minstrel black-face emerged, doing a racy little banjo number that incorporated antiquated terms like *darky* and *Negro*. A number of back-up dancers were dressed as wild tribesman, pretending to eat oversized, plastic slices of watermelon. And the kids watching in

KITTEN

the hall were rolling on the ground and wiping tears from their eyes.

Willoughby leaned over and spoke into Swann's ear: "I don't get it."

"Ah, young people's humor," the old man said, only to look at the screen and burst out with a laugh like a seal bark seconds later. There was an image of a pickaninny boy complete with rope belt, jet black skin, wide eyes, and sticky-out braided hair with ribbons on the ends. He marched zombie-like toward the camera.

"I don't get the humor of this world at all," the kitten huffed.

Tamanney managed to stop laughing long enough to say, "The Black boy is Schlege." Then he went right back to laughing. But, thank the Lord God, that was the end of the show.

Suddenly, the room rumbled with a timpani roll and a bright spotlight shone on a stage, illuminating a preteen girl dressed in a garish satin nightgown and a blazing plastic tiara. "Girls and boys, I have the proud pride of saying that I give you now the one, the only, the King!" She swooped her arms dramatically toward a tattered red velvet curtain being drawn slowly upward, accompanied by squeaks of unoiled pulleys. Slowly, a dais was revealed. Atop it, sitting on a throne, was a pudgy, baby-faced man with striking red hair plastered to his scalp. He wore the neon-green robes of child royalty and peered around at the audience with eerie gray eyes. Playfully, he articulated a realistic marionette of a young boy with a deadened face.

"Are you not feeling so well today, little Scottie?" The King asked in a comically concerned tone, like a mother in an old movie where everything turns out okay in the end. And then in bad ventriloquist fashion, with lips twitching, he made the little boy open his eyes and say, "No, sir. I don't feel so well at all."

Willoughby could discern that strings were affixed to the puppet's eyelids with small fishhooks, and it looked as though there was blood crusted around the areas where the hooks penetrated whatever served as its skin. But Tamanney beat him to the realization and blurted out, "Dear Lord God! He's using a dead boy as a puppet!" Swann sucked his teeth and shook his head, and several irritated surrounding children shushed Tamanney. He was right, of course; Willoughby could see that now.

The King continued, "If you aren't feeling well, I won't make you perform your jig." He lolled the boy's head around, as if the child were seasick and looking to puke over a gunwale. "I must perform my jig, sir. It is my function!" the marionette insisted, then proceeded to jerk about spastically as the King grinned and hummed some kind of oom-pah music. The hooks that affixed the strings began to tear at the boy's eyelids and lips as the dance became more frantic, with arms wind-milling and legs flailing. Once the King realized his toy was coming apart, he lifted the boy completely off the ground and tossed him to the side, so far that he cleared the dais and fell to the lower stage where the young girl still stood, attentively watching the King. All the children in the audience applauded, and Willoughby thought he could make out bits and pieces of their critiques, all seeming to indicate it was the King's best work yet.

The young girl once again faced the audience and shouted, "Down to business. It's court, guys!"

The children all chanted "Court, court, court!" and pumped their fists like they were at an AC/DC concert during the intro to *Thunderstruck*. A toddler, dressed in traditional English schoolboy garb, pranced around

KITTEN

the front of the stage, alternately playing air guitar and throwing dirty underwear into the audience. Small hands fought over each soiled brief, each stained boxer, leading only to more fist pumping and cheering.

"Is it me," Willoughby asked, "or is this getting a little Kafkaesque?"

"That is a mighty obscure reference for a small kitten to be making," Tamanney muttered, angry that he had not thought to make the comment first.

"If you ask me," Swann injected, "I'd say it's a bit more like the stranger moments of Gogol coupled with the more humorous passages of Borges."

"We didn't ask you, Captain!" snapped Tamanney, knowing full well the old sailor was correct.

And I'd like to add that maybe there's Donald Barthelme and Guy Maddin there, too.

The King clapped his hands. "Court is in session. Who has business for the King?"

"This is our chance!" Tamanney, with Willoughby on his shoulder, edged his way to the front, Capt. Swann not far behind.

"Ah?" said the King, tenting his fingers and applying full scrutiny to the three wayfarers. "You are not children, are you not not?"

The question was badly worded, and Tamanney pounced on it, handing the King a Double Negative card and attempting to argue some moot point that Willoughby didn't acknowledge. The kitten's attention had been distracted by a sudden, albeit slight, movement at the side of the stage. It was the boy-marionette. His eyes were flicking partly open, and he moved his hand slightly, as if to prop himself up in an attempt to stand. The arm gave way, unable to support any weight, and the child simply rolled his head from side to side. The kitten gave a small gasp, but did not cry out so as not to draw the attention of Tamanney, who really did have a gentle soul despite his crusty exterior. Willoughby wanted to spare the man the pain of knowing the child was only *mostly* dead.

"Enough!" The King stood and shook his finger at Tamanney, like the mother in an old movie where everything comes out right in the end. "We have been waiting for you three. Extos! Hexeram! Come forth!" From the left and right side of the stage emerged two young boys, both wearing dark capes and too-large motorcycle helmets. They looked like bobble-heads as they clunked forward to stand in front of the dais, one roughly in front of Tamanney, the other roughly in front of Capt. Swann. From beneath their capes, they produced, respectively, a power drill and a glass containing a big toe and a left ball.

"That—that is my power drill," said Tamanney. "But my neighbors borrowed that from me last year and never gave it back!"

"And that's my toe and testis!" shouted Swann. "What's the gig here?"

But it was too late; the boys lunged forward with childlike speed and impaled both men on the long daggers in their other hands. Willoughby was knocked to the ground, but being a kitten he managed to land on all fours. Removing their helmets, the two lads revealed their faces.

"The neighbor boy!"

"The powder monkey!"

Willoughby screamed as he watched his only friends double over, hands on their wounds like they could push the blood back in. The gallery of children roared with rage, or amusement, or satisfaction. Perhaps they roared for no reason but that they thought it was a funny thing to do while two men lay dying. An undead golf-clap came from the throne, and this enraged Willoughby the most.

KITTEN

"Why did you do this?" he demanded of the King.

"These men have wronged the children. I will not allow my subjects to be victimized." A groan came from the dying puppet-boy, barely audible above the gasping and grunting of Tamanney and Swann. Rushing to the side of Swann, who was already coughing up blood, Willoughby said, "I'm sorry you came ashore with us, Captain. It's all my fault!"

"Ah, kitten lad, it *is* your fault, but don't be sorry. I was the one who made the unwholesome advances on the powder monkey. He was just trying to do his job, deliver bundles of gunpowder so we could shoot our guns, and I had to take things one step too far and shoot off me own gun. Now, I suppose he'll cut off me other ball just for the sake of balance." The boy thought this was a good idea and did just that, adding the other testicle to the jar. Swann fainted from blood loss.

"Willoughby! Come here," said Tamanney quietly. The kitten approached the man's head sullenly, stopping only when his moist nose touched his cheek, and stood transfixed, waiting for him to speak. "Willoughby... I am your father."

"Huh?"

"It's true."

"But I'm a kitten."

"Maybe not your father spermwise, but I am your spiritual father here on the Steel Planet. Say it is so!" Tamanney's voice was weak and breathy. It was hard to listen to.

"Yes, father," Willoughby indulged him.

"And... and I wish to tell you my true name before I pass. Come closer."

"My nose is already touching your face."

"My... my true name is... is... arghhh..." And there

was a long moment where everyone thought Tamanney had died without revealing his true name, but then he spat out a nasty globule of bloody mucus and said, "My name is Willoughby," and he died.

Willoughby stared at him. "What the fuck?" He looked to Swann then, but the lights had gone out of his eyes as well. Then he turned to the King. "What the fucking fuck?"

The girl in the nightgown and tiara sniffed the air. "I smell dead fish," she said. For the life of him, Willoughby could not determine which man the smell had come from.

The King clapped twice to garner the attention of the on-looking masses. "Bury them. We don't want the throne room all stunk up." He turned to the girl, "Prophetess, what have you to say on this momentary occasion?"

The girl sniffed again and looked down on the bloody scene as children scrabbled to drag the corpses out. "My vibes are telling me, you are going to need a big old loaf of laundry soap." A chirping laugh issued from the King who slapped his knees and struggled to keep his breath. The last of the pall-bearing kids having exited, the King finally stopped laughing and the general susurrus of the crowd died to nothing. Suddenly, as if seized by a moment of clarity, the Prophetess cried out, "Lo! I see a boy. He's a nerd of indeterminate age. He wants something... He misses his kitten."

The King, regaining an ounce of decorum, sat back on his throne and smoothed the fabric of his toga. "Now that the first order of business is done, kitten, why do you come before me?"

Willoughby was weeping, yet he did manage to remember why he had come and what he must do. Swann's plan. Just ask the questions. "Is there any way for me to return to the world I came from?"

KITTEN

The King's laughter was full of disdain. "Kitten, do you believe that things are as they seem?"

It sounded like quite a non sequitur, but Willoughby played along: "Not always?"

"Very rarely, if ever," the King corrected. "By way of example, all these children here in the audience are nothing more than cardboard cutouts of children and you've been looking at them from their fronts. If you just adjust your angle a bit, you'll see they are two dimensional."

This struck Willoughby as ludicrous, but nonetheless he shifted position just enough to test the depth of the children that surrounded him, and found that they were, in fact, only cardboard cutouts. "But they were moving around a minute ago!"

"Were they?" asked the King. "Or was that purely in your mind?"

Incredulously, the kitten protested: "The boy that was jumping around like a coked-up monkey making armpit farts! He can't be just a cutout!"

After a long smirk, the King assented, "Yes, he was not a cardboard cutout. He was a real monkey on cocaine, and he was actually farting." He waved his hand to point out in the crowd amongst all the cutouts a monkey, jumping up and down and breaking wind like there was no tomorrow. "He is the one case in which things are exactly as they seem, proving the rule."

"But what does this mean? Can I go home or not?"

"Ah, if you really want to go home, I must show you into my Inner Rectum. It is a hallowed place."

Willoughby shivered at the idea of being forced into another orifice. "I don't think I want to go there."

The Prophetess, who appeared not to be cardboard, said, "It's gonna be great. I swear."

"No, no!"

G. Arthur Brown

The King of Children stood and removed his robe. Willoughby became nervous until he saw that the King had a small door in chest, something like a safe. After fiddling with the knob, the door opened, revealing a tunnel. "In you go, kitten. You leave us no choice now. Third double negative. To the Room of Questions!"

"But the second double negative was yours, not mine!"

The Prophetess scooped Willoughby up in her hands and carried him to the King as he clawed at her. "Believe in yourself and remember everything I told you," she said. "Remember my birthday. Remember some things I didn't even tell you." Then she stuffed him into the tunnel.

CHAPTER TWELVE

The tunnel was moist and completely dark. Willoughby thought it would never end, when suddenly, like a television set powering on, he was just *in* a room. It was the dorm room of a stoner, or maybe it was the Holy of Holies in an ancient temple, but filled with video game gear and bongs. A college-age kid with severe acne, dressed in a ball cap and grimy t-shirt that said "Chunder Lord" on it, spun around in his swivel chair and said, "Congrats, bruh! You beat the game, man!"

Willoughby, still trying to process his surroundings, merely said, "I did?"

"Yah, bruh! You totally found it all out! You just gotta, like, believe that you are gonna go home and like, yah, shit, bruh!"

"I just have to believe, that's all?"

"Yeah, well. *And* you have to kill yourself, but that's no sweat." The Chunder Lord took of his cap, then began to peel away the skin from his face, until a different face was revealed. The face of the long-haired, street-corner messiah. "Ride this plane right through the center of your soul." He held up a capsule. Then he put the torn skin back on his face, returned the cap to his head and said, "You just gotta believe in yourself, dude!"

Willoughby stared at the capsule in the Chunder Lord's fingers. Poison, evidently. He tried to make sense of it. If the world he came from was the World of the Dead, then dying would take him back there. But if he was wrong, then he would simply be killing himself, and dead might just be dead. "What will the capsule do?" he asked.

The Chunder Lord grinned wickedly. "It will make you throw up everything that is in you, including your *self*, which needs to be sent back home. But that is not what's important. Believe. *Believe.*"

Either he was joining a cult, or he was going to die. That seemed just about right to Willoughby, so he opened his mouth and allowed the Chunder Lord to place the capsule in it. He swallowed the capsule and drifted off into a smeary haze in which a montage of some of his favorite moments was replayed in super-psychedelic renditions. Then he saw the kinderwhore face of the Prophetess saying, "Poor kitty. You miss your Mommy. Come home to Mommy." And then she was dressed in Nanarina's cat suit, face obscured inside a huge red cat head. Willoughby weakly, dazedly stuck his paw out in an effort to keep her away. But she simply giggled and removed the cat head, revealing the slightly drugged visage of Amaand. "Come to Mommy!"

Willoughby screamed at the thought of being embraced, *being mothered*, by his stated archenemy, but then there was just a perfect blackness...

PART THREE:

THE END

Trevor was watching the latest episode of *Pirate Piet*. His mother was kind enough, or non-present enough, to allow him to eat sugary cereal right in front of the TV set. Piet was singing a song that explained what each part of the ship is called—the keel, the prow, the gooseneck, the bilge, the mizzenmast. The boy was a huge fan of the show, but not particularly inclined to adopt nautical terminology into his everyday vocabulary. He changed all the words in the song to *kitten*, and sang loudly after he finished drinking the sweet, multi-colored milk left over in his bowl. "Kitten, kitten, kitten! Yo ho ho ho ho!"

"Trevor! What are you going on about in there?" Amaand called from the kitchen.

A hollow feeling overtook him as he tried to find words to express how he felt to his mother. "Mommy. I miss my kitten. That's all." She walked into the family room with a forced look of concern upon her face.

"Aw, baby. You know that the kitten is in a better place. We talked about that. Kitten Heaven is like Disney World and Pirate Piet's ship rolled into one."

"I miss Willoughby!" he cried.

"I didn't know you had named that thing," said Amaand, smoothing his hair back.

"I had a dream. There was a crazy place full of crazy people, and my kitten was there and he was alive!"

"Now, Trevor, you know that this man killed your kitten." She motioned to the corpse of the Collector, still on the floor of the family room, but strangely well preserved. She didn't know what to do with the body. You can't exactly leave a cadaver out for garbage collection, and her husband, who would have otherwise handled this kind of thing, was still estranged.

As if on cue, the body began to twitch. Amaand staggered back and grabbed hold of her son. The mouth, stiff with rigor mortis, cracked open to reveal a kitten. But it was not a kitten, but more like a squirrel with long claws. Squirming itself free, it stared at Amaand. It ran toward her, serpentine, and began clawing at her shoes. "What the hell?" she said, reaching down to pick up the kitten by the scruff of its neck. It jerked stupidly and flailed futilely, but would not give up its attempts to scratch and scathe.

"Willoughby!" cried Trevor, taking the kitten and holding it in his arms. But the kitten struggled to escape, lurching in the direction of Amaand, then vomiting a stamp from Romania that featured a red cat.

"Oh! He misses his Mommy!" said Trevor, who gave it one last nuzzle before returning it to Amaand.

"Yeah, great. We are just one big happy family again." There was a sadness in her voice that Trevor didn't understand. She held the thing in a prone position to avoid being scratched and rocked it like she had done with Trevor as a baby. It wiggled, like a beetle on its back, but finally settled down and drifted off to sleep.

The telephone rang, and Trevor raced to pick it up. "Hello, Daddy! My kitten is home!"

"That's great to hear, son," his father said. "Tell your mother you'll take good care of the kitten so she doesn't worry. You know how she gets."

"Okay, Daddy. When can I see you?"

KITTEN

"Oh, well... you'll have to ask your mother about that. Goodbye, sunshine."

"Goodbye, Daddy! I love you." Then looking at the television set, Trevor cried, "Ooo! The new episode of *Mungus the Republican Dog*!"

Amaand gazed curiously at the kitten, wondering what the thing actually was and what it wanted and where it had been for the last few days. Inside the Collector's stomach?

The dead girl entered the room, wearing a white t-shirt that said *Big Fun* in bold black letters.

"Hi, Sissy!" shouted Trevor.

Amaand simpered and said, "Look who has rejoined us! I wondered where you had got off to."

The dead girl flashed her perfect teeth at the kitten. She turned toward the audience and held up a handwritten sign that said "This story is over."

G. ARTHUR BROWN cannot be biographied for reasons literary science has yet to explain. He was purportedly sighted recently, burrito in hand, outside a Qdoba, putting to bed rumors that he cannot be seen with the naked eye. Biographers, it seems, will just have to try much harder in future.

Bizarro Books

CATALOG SPRING 2012

ERASERHEAD PRESS

Swallowdown Press

FunGasm

LAZY FASCIST

Your major resource for the bizarro fiction genre:
WWW.BIZARROCENTRAL.COM

Introduce yourselves to the bizarro fiction genre and all of its authors with the Bizarro Starter Kit series. Each volume features short novels and short stories by ten of the leading bizarro authors, designed to give you a perfect sampling of the genre for only $10.

BB-0X1
"The Bizarro Starter Kit"
(Orange)
Featuring D. Harlan Wilson, Carlton Mellick III, Jeremy Robert Johnson, Kevin L Donihe, Gina Ranalli, Andre Duza, Vincent W. Sakowski, Steve Beard, John Edward Lawson, and Bruce Taylor. **236 pages $10**

BB-0X2
"The Bizarro Starter Kit"
(Blue)
Featuring Ray Fracalossy, Jeremy C. Shipp, Jordan Krall, Mykle Hansen, Andersen Prunty, Eckhard Gerdes, Bradley Sands, Steve Aylett, Christian TeBordo, and Tony Rauch. **244 pages $10**

BB-0X2
"The Bizarro Starter Kit"
(Purple)
Featuring Russell Edson, Athena Villaverde, David Agranoff, Matthew Revert, Andrew Goldfarb, Jeff Burk, Garrett Cook, Kris Saknussemm, Cody Goodfellow, and Cameron Pierce **264 pages $10**

BB-001 "The Kafka Effekt" D. Harlan Wilson — A collection of forty-four irreal short stories loosely written in the vein of Franz Kafka, with more than a pinch of William S. Burroughs sprinkled on top. **211 pages $14**

BB-002 "Satan Burger" Carlton Mellick III — The cult novel that put Carlton Mellick III on the map ... Six punks get jobs at a fast food restaurant owned by the devil in a city violently overpopulated by surreal alien cultures. **236 pages $14**

BB-003 "Some Things Are Better Left Unplugged" Vincent Sakwoski — Join The Man and his Nemesis, the obese tabby, for a nightmare roller coaster ride into this postmodern fantasy. **152 pages $10**

BB-004 "Shall We Gather At the Garden?" Kevin L Donihe — Donihe's Debut novel. Midgets take over the world, The Church of Lionel Richie vs. The Church of the Byrds, plant porn and more! **244 pages $14**

BB-005 "Razor Wire Pubic Hair" Carlton Mellick III — A genderless humandildo is purchased by a razor dominatrix and brought into her nightmarish world of bizarre sex and mutilation. **176 pages $11**

BB-006 "Stranger on the Loose" D. Harlan Wilson — The fiction of Wilson's 2nd collection is planted in the soil of normalcy, but what grows out of that soil is a dark, witty, otherworldly jungle... **228 pages $14**

BB-007 "The Baby Jesus Butt Plug" Carlton Mellick III — Using clones of the Baby Jesus for anal sex will be the hip sex fetish of the future. **92 pages $10**

BB-008 "Fishyfleshed" Carlton Mellick III — The world of the past is an illogical flatland lacking in dimension and color, a sick-scape of crispy squid people wandering the desert for no apparent reason. **260 pages $14**

BB-009 "**Dead Bitch Army**" **Andre Duza** — Step into a world filled with racist teenagers, cannibals, 100 warped Uncle Sams, automobiles with razor-sharp teeth, living graffiti, and a pissed-off zombie bitch out for revenge. **344 pages $16**

BB-010 "**The Menstruating Mall**" **Carlton Mellick III** — "The Breakfast Club meets Chopping Mall as directed by David Lynch." - Brian Keene **212 pages $12**

BB-011 "**Angel Dust Apocalypse**" **Jeremy Robert Johnson** — Methheads, man-made monsters, and murderous Neo-Nazis. "Seriously amazing short stories..." - Chuck Palahniuk, author of Fight Club **184 pages $11**

BB-012 "**Ocean of Lard**" **Kevin L Donihe / Carlton Mellick III** — A parody of those old Choose Your Own Adventure kid's books about some very odd pirates sailing on a sea made of animal fat. **176 pages $12**

BB-015 "**Foop!**" **Chris Genoa** — Strange happenings are going on at Dactyl, Inc, the world's first and only time travel tourism company.
"A surreal pie in the face!" - Christopher Moore   **300 pages $14**

BB-020 "**Punk Land**" **Carlton Mellick III** — In the punk version of Heaven, the anarchist utopia is threatened by corporate fascism and only Goblin, Mortician's sperm, and a blue-mohawked female assassin named Shark Girl can stop them. **284 pages $15**

BB-027 "**Siren Promised**" **Jeremy Robert Johnson & Alan M Clark** — Nominated for the Bram Stoker Award. A potent mix of bad drugs, bad dreams, brutal bad guys, and surreal/incredible art by Alan M. Clark. **190 pages $13**

BB-031"**Sea of the Patchwork Cats**" **Carlton Mellick III** — A quiet dreamlike tale set in the ashes of the human race. For Mellick enthusiasts who also adore The Twilight Zone. **112 pages $10**

BB-032 "Extinction Journals" Jeremy Robert Johnson — An uncanny voyage across a newly nuclear America where one man must confront the problems associated with loneliness, insane dieties, radiation, love, and an ever-evolving cockroach suit with a mind of its own. **104 pages $10**

BB-037 "The Haunted Vagina" Carlton Mellick III — It's difficult to love a woman whose vagina is a gateway to the world of the dead. **132 pages $10**

BB-043 "War Slut"   Carlton Mellick III   — Part "1984," part "Waiting for Godot," and part action horror video game adaptation of John Carpenter's "The Thing." **116 pages $10**

BB-047 "Sausagey Santa"   Carlton Mellick III — A bizarro Christmas tale featuring Santa as a piratey mutant with a body made of sausages. **124 pages $10**

BB-048 "Misadventures in a Thumbnail Universe" Vincent Sakowski — Dive deep into the surreal and satirical realms of neo-classical Blender Fiction, filled with television shoes and flesh-filled skies. **120 pages $10**

BB-053 "Ballad of a Slow Poisoner" Andrew Goldfarb — Millford Mutterwurst sat down on a Tuesday to take his afternoon tea, and made the unpleasant discovery that his elbows were becoming flatter. **128 pages $10**

BB-055 "Help! A Bear is Eating Me" Mykle Hansen — The bizarro, heartwarming, magical tale of poor planning, hubris and severe blood loss... **150 pages $11**

BB-056 "Piecemeal June" Jordan Krall — A man falls in love with a living sex doll, but with love comes danger when her creator comes after her with crab-squid assassins. **90 pages $9**

BB-058 "The Overwhelming Urge" Andersen Prunty — A collection of bizarro tales by Andersen Prunty. **150 pages $11**

BB-059 "Adolf in Wonderland" Carlton Mellick III — A dreamlike adventure that takes a young descendant of Adolf Hitler's design and sends him down the rabbit hole into a world of imperfection and disorder. **180 pages $11**

BB-061 "Ultra Fuckers" Carlton Mellick III — Absurdist suburban horror about a couple who enter an upper middle class gated community but can't find their way out. **108 pages $9**

BB-062 "House of Houses" Kevin L. Donihe — An odd man wants to marry his house. Unfortunately, all of the houses in the world collapse at the same time in the Great House Holocaust. Now he must travel to House Heaven to find his departed fiancee. **172 pages $11**

BB-064 "Squid Pulp Blues" Jordan Krall — In these three bizarro-noir novellas, the reader is thrown into a world of murderers, drugs made from squid parts, deformed gun-toting veterans, and a mischievous apocalyptic donkey. **204 pages $12**

BB-065 "Jack and Mr. Grin" Andersen Prunty — "When Mr. Grin calls you can hear a smile in his voice. Not a warm and friendly smile, but the kind that seizes your spine in fear. You don't need to pay your phone bill to hear it. That smile is in every line of Prunty's prose." - Tom Bradley. **208 pages $12**

BB-066 "Cybernetrix" Carlton Mellick III — What would you do if your normal everyday world was slowly mutating into the video game world from Tron? **212 pages $12**

BB-072 "Zerostrata" Andersen Prunty — Hansel Nothing lives in a tree house, suffers from memory loss, has a very eccentric family, and falls in love with a woman who runs naked through the woods every night. **144 pages $11**

BB-073 "The Egg Man" Carlton Mellick III — It is a world where humans reproduce like insects. Children are the property of corporations, and having an enormous ten-foot brain implanted into your skull is a grotesque sexual fetish. Mellick's industrial urban dystopia is one of his darkest and grittiest to date. **184 pages $11**

BB-074 "Shark Hunting in Paradise Garden" Cameron Pierce — A group of strange humanoid religious fanatics travel back in time to the Garden of Eden to discover it is invested with hundreds of giant flying maneating sharks. **150 pages $10**

BB-075 "Apeshit" Carlton Mellick III - Friday the 13th meets Visitor Q. Six hipster teens go to a cabin in the woods inhabited by a deformed killer. An incredibly fucked-up parody of B-horror movies with a bizarro slant. **192 pages $12**

BB-076 "Fuckers of Everything on the Crazy Shitting Planet of the Vomit Atmosphere" Mykle Hansen - Three bizarro satires. Monster Cocks, Journey to the Center of Agnes Cuddlebottom, and Crazy Shitting Planet. **228 pages $12**

BB-077 "The Kissing Bug" Daniel Scott Buck — In the tradition of Roald Dahl, Tim Burton, and Edward Gorey, comes this bizarro anti-war children's story about a bohemian conenose kissing bug who falls in love with a human woman. **116 pages $10**

BB-078 "MachoPoni" Lotus Rose — It's My Little Pony... *Bizarro* style! A long time ago Poniworld was split in two. On one side of the Jagged Line is the Pastel Kingdom, a magical land of music, parties, and positivity. On the other side of the Jagged Line is Dark Kingdom inhabited by an army of undead ponies. **148 pages $11**

BB-079 "The Faggiest Vampire" Carlton Mellick III — A Roald Dahl-esque children's story about two faggy vampires who partake in a mustache competition to find out which one is truly the faggiest. **104 pages $10**

BB-080 "Sky Tongues" Gina Ranalli — The autobiography of Sky Tongues, the biracial hermaphrodite actress with tongues for fingers. Follow her strange life story as she rises from freak to fame. **204 pages $12**

BB-081 "Washer Mouth" Kevin L. Donihe - A washing machine becomes human and pursues his dream of meeting his favorite soap opera star. **244 pages $11**

BB-082 "Shatnerquake" Jeff Burk - All of the characters ever played by William Shatner are suddenly sucked into our world. Their mission: hunt down and destroy the real William Shatner. **100 pages $10**

BB-083 "The Cannibals of Candyland" Carlton Mellick III - There exists a race of cannibals that are made of candy. They live in an underground world made out of candy. One man has dedicated his life to killing them all. **170 pages $11**

BB-084 "Slub Glub in the Weird World of the Weeping Willows" Andrew Goldfarb - The charming tale of a blue glob named Slub Glub who helps the weeping willows whose tears are flooding the earth. There are also hyenas, ghosts, and a voodoo priest **100 pages $10**

BB-085 "Super Fetus" Adam Pepper - Try to abort this fetus and he'll kick your ass! **104 pages $10**

BB-086 "Fistful of Feet" Jordan Krall - A bizarro tribute to spaghetti westerns, featuring Cthulhu-worshipping Indians, a woman with four feet, a crazed gunman who is obsessed with sucking on candy, Syphilis-ridden mutants, sexually transmitted tattoos, and a house devoted to the freakiest fetishes. **228 pages $12**

BB-087 "Ass Goblins of Auschwitz" Cameron Pierce - It's Monty Python meets Nazi exploitation in a surreal nightmare as can only be imagined by Bizarro author Cameron Pierce. **104 pages $10**

BB-088 "Silent Weapons for Quiet Wars" Cody Goodfellow - "This is high-end psychological surrealist horror meets bottom-feeding low-life crime in a techno-thrilling science fiction world full of Lovecraft and magic..." -John Skipp **212 pages $12**

BB-089 "Warrior Wolf Women of the Wasteland" Carlton Mellick III — Road Warrior Werewolves versus McDonaldland Mutants...post-apocalyptic fiction has never been quite like this. **316 pages $13**

BB-091 "Super Giant Monster Time" Jeff Burk — A tribute to choose your own adventures and Godzilla movies. Will you escape the giant monsters that are rampaging the fuck out of your city and shit? Or will you join the mob of alien-controlled punk rockers causing chaos in the streets? What happens next depends on you. **188 pages $12**

BB-092 "Perfect Union" Cody Goodfellow — "Cronenberg's THE FLY on a grand scale: human/insect gene-spliced body horror, where the human hive politics are as shocking as the gore." -John Skipp. **272 pages $13**

BB-093 "Sunset with a Beard" Carlton Mellick III — 14 stories of surreal science fiction. **200 pages $12**

BB-094 **"My Fake War" Andersen Prunty** — The absurd tale of an unlikely soldier forced to fight a war that, quite possibly, does not exist. It's Rambo meets Waiting for Godot in this subversive satire of American values and the scope of the human imagination. **128 pages $11**

BB-095 **"Lost in Cat Brain Land" Cameron Pierce** — Sad stories from a surreal world. A fascist mustache, the ghost of Franz Kafka, a desert inside a dead cat. Primordial entities mourn the death of their child. The desperate serve tea to mysterious creatures. A hopeless romantic falls in love with a pterodactyl. And much more. **152 pages $11**

BB-096 **"The Kobold Wizard's Dildo of Enlightenment +2" Carlton Mellick III** — A Dungeons and Dragons parody about a group of people who learn they are only made up characters in an AD&D campaign and must find a way to resist their nerdy teenaged players and retarded dungeon master in order to survive. **232 pages $12**

BB-098 **"A Hundred Horrible Sorrows of Ogner Stump" Andrew Goldfarb** — Goldfarb's acclaimed comic series. A magical and weird journey into the horrors of everyday life. **164 pages $11**

BB-099 "Pickled Apocalypse of Pancake Island" Cameron Pierce—A demented fairy tale about a pickle, a pancake, and the apocalypse. **102 pages $8**

BB-100 "Slag Attack" Andersen Prunty— Slag Attack features four visceral, noir stories about the living, crawling apocalypse.A slag is what survivors are calling the slug-like maggots raining from the sky, burrowing inside people, and hollowing out their flesh and their sanity. **148 pages $11**

BB-101 "Slaughterhouse High" Robert Devereaux—A place where schools are built with secret passageways, rebellious teens get zippers installed in their mouths and genitals, and once a year, on that special night, one couple is slaughtered and the bits of their bodies are kept as souvenirs. **304 pages $13**

BB-102 "The Emerald Burrito of Oz" John Skipp & Marc Levinthal —OZ IS REAL! Magic is real! The gate is really in Kansas! And America is finally allowing Earth tourists to visit this weird-ass, mysterious land. But when Gene of Los Angeles heads off for summer vacation in the Emerald City, little does he know that a war is brewing...a war that could destroy both worlds. **280 pages $13**

BB-103 "The Vegan Revolution... with Zombies" David Agranoff — When there's no more meat in hell, the vegans will walk the earth. **160 pages $11**

BB-104 "The Flappy Parts" Kevin L Donihe—Poems about bunnies, LSD, and police abuse. You know, things that matter. 132 **pages $11**

BB-105 "Sorry I Ruined Your Orgy" Bradley Sands—Bizarro humorist Bradley Sands returns with one of the strangest, most hilarious collections of the year. **130 pages $11**

BB-106 "Mr. Magic Realism" Bruce Taylor—Like Golden Age science fiction comics written by Freud, *Mr. Magic Realism* is a strange, insightful adventure that spans the furthest reaches of the galaxy, exploring the hidden caverns in the hearts and minds of men, women, aliens, and biomechanical cats. **152 pages $11**

BB-107 "Zombies and Shit" Carlton Mellick III—"Battle Royale" meets "Return of the Living Dead." Mellick's bizarro tribute to the zombie genre. **308 pages $13**

BB-108 "The Cannibal's Guide to Ethical Living" Mykle Hansen— Over a five star French meal of fine wine, organic vegetables and human flesh, a lunatic delivers a witty, chilling, disturbingly sane argument in favor of eating the rich.. **184 pages $11**

BB-109 "Starfish Girl" Athena Villaverde—In a post-apocalyptic underwater dome society, a girl with a starfish growing from her head and an assassin with sea anenome hair are on the run from a gang of mutant fish men. **160 pages $11**

BB-110 "Lick Your Neighbor" Chris Genoa—Mutant ninjas, a talking whale, kung fu masters, maniacal pilgrims, and an alcoholic clown populate Chris Genoa's surreal, darkly comical and unnerving reimagining of the first Thanksgiving. **303 pages $13**

BB-111 "Night of the Assholes" Kevin L. Donihe—A plague of assholes is infecting the countryside. Normal everyday people are transforming into jerks, snobs, dicks, and douchebags. And they all have only one purpose: to make your life a living hell.. **192 pages $11**

BB-112 "Jimmy Plush, Teddy Bear Detective" Garrett Cook—Hardboiled cases of a private detective trapped within a teddy bear body. **180 pages $11**

BB-113 "The Deadheart Shelters" Forrest Armstrong—The hip hop lovechild of William Burroughs and Dali... **144 pages $11**

BB-114 "Eyeballs Growing All Over Me... Again" Tony Raugh— Absurd, surreal, playful, dream-like, whimsical, and a lot of fun to read. **144 pages $11**

BB-115 "Whargoul" Dave Brockie — From the killing grounds of Stalingrad to the death camps of the holocaust. From torture chambers in Iraq to race riots in the United States, the Whargoul was there, killing and raping. **244 pages $12**

BB-116 "By the Time We Leave Here, We'll Be Friends" J. David Osborne — A David Lynchian nightmare set in a Russian gulag, where its prisoners, guards, traitors, soldiers, lovers, and demons fight for survival and their own rapidly deteriorating humanity. **168 pages $11**

BB-117 "Christmas on Crack" edited by Carlton Mellick III — Perverted Christmas Tales for the whole family! . . . as long as every member of your family is over the age of 18. **168 pages $11**

BB-118 "Crab Town" Carlton Mellick III — Radiation fetishists, balloon people, mutant crabs, sail-bike road warriors, and a love affair between a woman and an H-Bomb. This is one mean asshole of a city. Welcome to Crab Town. **100 pages $8**

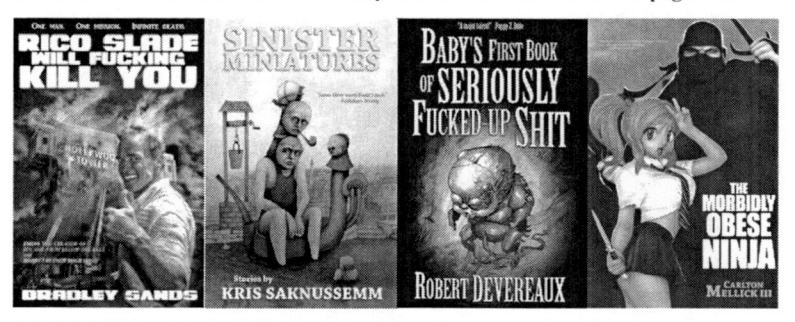

BB-119 "Rico Slade Will Fucking Kill You" Bradley Sands — Rico Slade is an action hero. Rico Slade can rip out a throat with his bare hands. Rico Slade's favorite food is the honey-roasted peanut. Rico Slade will fucking kill everyone. A novel. **122 pages $8**

BB-120 "Sinister Miniatures" Kris Saknussemm — The definitive collection of short fiction by Kris Saknussemm, confirming that he is one of the best, most daring writers of the weird to emerge in the twenty-first century. **180 pages $11**

BB-121 "Baby's First Book of Seriously Fucked up Shit" Robert Devereaux — Ten stories of the strange, the gross, and the just plain fucked up from one of the most original voices in horror. **176 pages $11**

BB-122 "The Morbidly Obese Ninja" Carlton Mellick III — These days, if you want to run a successful company . . . you're going to need a lot of ninjas. **92 pages $8**

BB-123 "Abortion Arcade" Cameron Pierce — An intoxicating blend of body horror and midnight movie madness, reminiscent of early David Lynch and the splatterpunks at their most sublime. **172 pages $11**
BB-124 "Black Hole Blues" Patrick Wensink — A hilarious double helix of country music and physics. **196 pages $11**
BB-125 "Barbarian Beast Bitches of the Badlands" Carlton Mellick III — Three prequels and sequels to *Warrior Wolf Women of the Wasteland*. **284 pages $13**
BB-126 "The Traveling Dildo Salesman" Kevin L. Donihe — A nightmare comedy about destiny, faith, and sex toys. Also featuring Donihe's most lurid and infamous short stories: *Milky Agitation, Two-Way Santa, The Helen Mower, Living Room Zombies*, and *Revenge of the Living Masturbation Rag*. **108 pages $8**

BB-127 "Metamorphosis Blues" Bruce Taylor — Enter a land of love beasts, intergalactic cowboys, and rock 'n roll. A land where Sears Catalogs are doorways to insanity and men keep mysterious black boxes. Welcome to the monstrous mind of Mr. Magic Realism. **136 pages $11**
BB-128 "The Driver's Guide to Hitting Pedestrians" Andersen Prunty — A pocket guide to the twenty-three most painful things in life, written by the most well-adjusted man in the universe. **108 pages $8**
BB-129 "Island of the Super People" Kevin Shamel — Four students and their anthropology professor journey to a remote island to study its indigenous population. But this is no ordinary native culture. They're super heroes and villains with flesh costumes and outlandish abilities like self-detonation, musical eyelashes, and microwave hands. **194 pages $11**
BB-130 "Fantastic Orgy" Carlton Mellick III — Shark Sex, mutant cats, and strange sexually transmitted diseases. Featuring the stories: *Candy-coated, Ear Cat, Fantastic Orgy, City Hobgoblins*, and *Porno in August*. **136 pages $9**

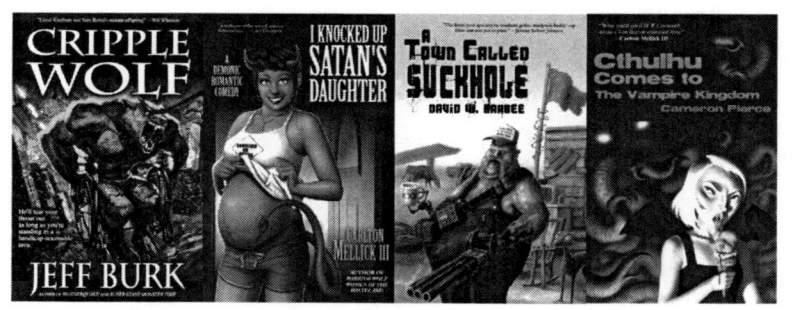

BB-131 **"Cripple Wolf" Jeff Burk** — Part man. Part wolf. 100% crippled. Also including *Punk Rock Nursing Home, Adrift with Space Badgers, Cook for Your Life, Just Another Day in the Park, Frosty and the Full Monty,* and *House of Cats.* **152 pages $10**

BB-132 **"I Knocked Up Satan's Daughter" Carlton Mellick III** — An adorable, violent, fantastical love story. A romantic comedy for the bizarro fiction reader. **152 pages $10**

BB-133 **"A Town Called Suckhole" David W. Barbee** — Far into the future, in the nuclear bowels of post-apocalyptic Dixie, there is a town. A town of derelict mobile homes, ancient junk, and mutant wildlife. A town of slack jawed rednecks who bask in the splendors of moonshine and mud boggin'. A town dedicated to the bloody and demented legacy of the Old South. A town called Suckhole. **144 pages $10**

BB-134 **"Cthulhu Comes to the Vampire Kingdom" Cameron Pierce** — What you'd get if H. P. Lovecraft wrote a Tim Burton animated film. **148 pages $11**

BB-135 **"I am Genghis Cum" Violet LeVoit** — From the savage Arctic tundra to post-partum mutations to your missing daughter's unmarked grave, join visionary madwoman Violet LeVoit in this non-stop eight-story onslaught of full-tilt Bizarro punk lit thrills. **124 pages $9**

BB-136 **"Haunt" Laura Lee Bahr** — A tripping-balls Los Angeles noir, where a mysterious dame drags you through a time-warping Bizarro hall of mirrors. **316 pages $13**

BB-137 **"Amazing Stories of the Flying Spaghetti Monster" edited by Cameron Pierce** — Like an all-spaghetti evening of Adult Swim, the Flying Spaghetti Monster will show you the many realms of His Noodly Appendage. Learn of those who worship him and the lives he touches in distant, mysterious ways. **228 pages $12**

BB-138 **"Wave of Mutilation" Douglas Lain** — A dream-pop exploration of modern architecture and the American identity, *Wave of Mutilation* is a Zen finger trap for the 21st century. **100 pages $8**

BB-139 "Hooray for Death!" Mykle Hansen — Famous Author Mykle Hansen draws unconventional humor from deaths tiny and large, and invites you to laugh while you can. **128 pages $10**

BB-140 "Hypno-hog's Moonshine Monster Jamboree" Andrew Goldfarb — Hicks, Hogs, Horror! Goldfarb is back with another strange illustrated tale of backwoods weirdness. **120 pages $9**

BB-141 "Broken Piano For President" Patrick Wensink — A comic masterpiece about the fast food industry, booze, and the necessity to choose happiness over work and security. **372 pages $15**

BB-142 "Please Do Not Shoot Me in the Face" Bradley Sands — A novel in three parts, *Please Do Not Shoot Me in the Face: A Novel*, is the story of one boy detective, the worst ninja in the world, and the great American fast food wars. It is a novel of loss, destruction, and--incredibly--genuine hope. **224 pages $12**

BB-143 "Santa Steps Out" Robert Devereaux — Sex, Death, and Santa Claus ... The ultimate erotic Christmas story is back. **294 pages $13**

BB-144 "Santa Conquers the Homophobes" Robert Devereaux — "I wish I could hope to ever attain one-thousandth the perversity of Robert Devereaux's toenail clippings." - Poppy Z. Brite **316 pages $13**

BB-145 "We Live Inside You" Jeremy Robert Johnson — "Jeremy Robert Johnson is dancing to a way different drummer. He loves language, he loves the edge, and he loves us people. These stories have range and style and wit. This is entertainment... and literature."- Jack Ketchum **188 pages $11**

BB-146 "Clockwork Girl" Athena Villaverde — Urban fairy tales for the weird girl in all of us. Like a combination of Francesca Lia Block, Charles de Lint, Kathe Koja, Tim Burton, and Hayao Miyazaki, her stories are cute, kinky, edgy, magical, provocative, and strange, full of poetic imagery and vicious sexuality. **160 pages $10**

BB-147 "Armadillo Fists" Carlton Mellick III — A weird-as-hell gangster story set in a world where people drive giant mechanical dinosaurs instead of cars. **168 pages $11**

BB-148 "Gargoyle Girls of Spider Island" Cameron Pierce — Four college seniors venture out into open waters for the tropical party weekend of a lifetime. Instead of a teenage sex fantasy, they find themselves in a nightmare of pirates, sharks, and sex-crazed monsters. **100 pages $8**

BB-149 "The Handsome Squirm" by Carlton Mellick III — Like Franz Kafka's *The Trial* meets an erotic body horror version of *The Blob*. **158 pages $11**

BB-150 "Tentacle Death Trip" Jordan Krall — It's *Death Race 2000* meets H. P. Lovecraft in bizarro author Jordan Krall's best and most suspenseful work to date. **224 pages $12**

BB-151 "The Obese" Nick Antosca — Like Alfred Hitchcock's *The Birds*... but with obese people. **108 pages $10**

BB-152 "All-Monster Action!" Cody Goodfellow — The world gave him a blank check and a demand: Create giant monsters to fight our wars. But Dr. Otaku was not satisfied with mere chaos and mass destruction.... **216 pages $12**

BB-153 "Ugly Heaven" Carlton Mellick III — Heaven is no longer a paradise. It was once a blissful utopia full of wonders far beyond human comprehension. But the afterlife is now in ruins. It has become an ugly, lonely wasteland populated by strange monstrous beasts, masturbating angels, and sad man-like beings wallowing in the remains of the once-great Kingdom of God. **106 pages $8**

BB-154 "Space Walrus" Kevin L. Donihe — Walter is supposed to go where no walrus has ever gone before, but all this astronaut walrus really wants is to take it easy on the intense training, escape the chimpanzee bullies, and win the love of his human trainer Dr. Stephanie. **160 pages $11**